Winning Ben

by

JoMarie DeGioia

PUBLISHED BY:

Bailey Park Publishing

Winning Ben

Book Four of the
Cypress Corners Series

by

JoMarie DeGioia

Chapter 1

Chapman Financial, Boston

Ben Chapman scratched his pen over the piece of scrap paper in front of him, desperate for an idea to strike. He thought about the projects he'd worked on back in Santa Cruz just a year ago. Beach houses and condo redesigns in the bright sunshine of that laid-back city. It felt more like a lifetime than a year ago, though. Of course, thinking back made him think about last Christmas. His last Christmas with his mother.

Shoving the paper aside, he twirled the pen between the fingers of his right hand. Turning back to the computer, he reviewed the documents his father sent him. Numbers and percentages and projections. He could read the patterns and see the value, but the entries held no interest for him.

He'd been working at Chapman since mid-summer. Now it was nearly September but he doubted he would last here through the end of the year. He couldn't seem to focus on any projects back in Cali since his mother died, so he'd packed up and moved to Boston. Of all places.

His father had all but begged him to make the move, which was astounding in itself. He'd never shown any real interest in

Ben up to that point last spring when he'd called and said he had something to tell him. Man, had that something been…something. He had two brothers and a sister he never knew about.

A sharp rap came at his door but his visitor didn't wait for him to answer. No. Bill Chapman strode into Ben's office just like he'd barreled back into his life.

"Ben," Bill said without preamble. "I need your help."

Ben deliberately put his pen back down on the desk and folded his hands. "Help with what?"

Bill stalked closer, his expression intense. It was his father's default expression, Ben was coming to recognize. How his free spirit of a mother had ever gotten tangled up with the tight-ass, he'd never know.

"I need your help down in Cypress."

Ben thought for a second. Cypress Corners, located in Central Florida, was one of Chapman's most successful projects. He'd been impressed during his short visit there over the summer. A sprawling property of ten thousand acres featuring upscale retail, state-of-the-art homes and an award-winning golf course, it was also the home of Ben's newfound siblings. That odd pang in his gut came, as it always did when he thought about the family he'd never known until now.

Ben sat back as he considered his father's words, taking in the man's appearance from head to toe. He was tall and broad and still handsome at his age. Ben took a lot of features from him. Bill's thick, dark hair and his build. When he'd met his brothers Rick and Jake several weeks ago he'd seen the resemblance among all three of them, too. It was weird, realizing he shared so much with those men yet he'd shared nothing with them all of his life.

Bill was dressed and pressed and the picture of the successful man he was. Chapman Financial backed numerous projects and their investors saw very satisfying returns. Even Ben could see that from the documents he'd reviewed this morning.

"What can you possibly need me for?" There was a weight in that question but his father seemed to ignore it. As usual.

"You're an architect."

Ben blew out a breath. He hadn't designed a damn thing in months and the title felt false. Fake. "And?"

Bill settled into the chair opposite. Ben's desk was huge, as was his office. He'd been told his brother Jake had occupied this space before him, when he'd flown in to work at Chapman for a couple of months a year. That was before he moved to Cypress for good, though. Just like Rick and their sister Cassie had. And now Bill needed him to head down there?

"The developers want to expand on their green homes, Ben. Which you know."

Ben shrugged. Cassie's fiancé Ty had mentioned that. "Yeah. I know."

"I want you to give your input on the designs." Bill paused, his gaze steady. "Chapman's input."

Ben's throat tightened. "I'm taking a break from designing."

Bill nodded as he waved a hand. "Yeah, so you've said. Listen, Ben. You were only down there for a couple of days this summer. You don't know how that place works. The tree-huggers at the Cypress Institute pretty much run the place and the developers have to work with them."

"I'm taking a break from designing," Ben said again.

"I need you on the inside. I want a hand in just how these new sections of the property are being planned and implemented."

"You want me to be your spy?" Ben smirked. "Should I wear a disguise?"

Bill shook his head. "No, no." His lips quirked in a smile.

"God, you remind me of your brother Jake."

Ben didn't know if that was true but he didn't mind the comparison. He'd gotten to know his siblings a little on that too-short visit. Jake was his daredevil brother who had settled down with the pretty redhead. He seemed like a pretty good guy too, and was just a year older than Ben's twenty-eight.

"I can't say anything to that. I don't really know my brother Jake."

Bill winced. Ben's statement hit his father just as he'd hoped it would. How the hell did a man keep the existence of another son from his children for twenty-eight years? And keep them from that son, too? Money was all Ben ever got from Bill Chapman. No attention. Certainly no affection.

That took a certain type of son-of-a-bitch and, from the few discussions he'd had with his siblings, Bill was just that particular kind.

"Yeah, well," Bill said. "Just head down there and get in good with the developers. With the sales staff and the Institute, too."

Ben picked up his pen, twirling it through his fingers again. "You know, it seems to me that Rick would be the perfect guy for the job. He runs the Sales Center and his wife works for the

Cypress Institute."

Bill ran a hand over his jaw, his gaze drifting over Ben's shoulder and out the wide glass windows at Ben's back. "Rick and I don't exactly..." He trailed off.

"Have a relationship? Yeah, I got that."

Bill cleared his throat. "Look. You're going down to Cypress for Cassandra's wedding next month, right?"

Ben nodded. "A couple of weeks before, actually."

His sister had insisted that Ben be a part of the celebration and he'd found he couldn't deny the little spitfire anything. It was odd, the beginnings of a connection he felt with all three of his siblings. He wondered just how close they all could have been if they'd grown up in each other's lives.

"Aren't you going down for the wedding?" he asked his father.

Again Bill looked away. "I'm not sure."

Ben let the subject drop. Whatever brand of crap went on between Bill and his other kids, Ben wasn't a part of that either. He thanked God for small favors as he considered his father's request. He suspected he had more in common with Rick, Jake and Cassie, too. It was worth trying to get to know them all better. Besides, there was nothing here for him in Boston. And there sure as hell was nothing left for him in Santa Cruz.

Ben stopped twirling the pen and nodded. "When do you need me there?"

***

Cypress Corners, Florida

Tammy Donato hummed to herself as she breezed back into the Sales Center, her heels clicking over the travertine tile floor with each step. The tour had gone like gangbusters and the group of prospective residents trailing in behind her was chatting and smiling and giving her every indication that she'd driven her points home this afternoon.

Cypress was a great place to live. She believed that, even if she didn't buy into the rest of it all. There were way too many references to kids and family in her spiel but she had to make those points. She supposed they were true. The schools were stellar and the recreation areas primed for families with kids of all ages.

"Will we see you at the picnic by the lake tonight, Tammy?" one of the women asked her.

No friggin' way. "You just might," Tammy said with a grin.

With a parting wave, Tammy disappeared into her office

before she could say just what she thought about the planned family-friendly activities that seemed to go on every single day in Cypress. There was no way in hell she was going to attend an event so full of sticky, noisy kids.

She sat in her chair and thumbed through the latest prospectus from her boss. More homes were planned, and she was just the girl to push them. Um, promote them. Green homes, with even more eco-advanced features than what was going on already. It was part of the Cypress Institute's mission for the property. Cypress Corners sat on ten thousand acres in Central Florida, and more than half of that was reserved for plant and animal conservation.

Oliver opened her door and strolled in. "Hey, girl." His blond hair was artfully tousled and his perfect features were beaming.

"Hey, Ollie."

Ollie cocked his head to the side, his full lips in a pout. "How are you going to get out of tonight's picnic?"

Tammy waved a hand. "Family stuff isn't in my wheelhouse, boy. I'll promote the events as fun, family entertainment but there's no way I'm going to any one of them. Besides, I usually take off for the beach on Fridays."

"I know." Ollie shook his head. "But that's not what Mr. Forbes says."

"What?"

"He says we should all go."

"He does?" Tammy bit back a favorite Italian curse of her father's as she shook her head. "Well, Mr. Forbes can—"

"Mr. Forbes can what?" Mr. Forbes asked, leaning in the doorway.

Her face flushed hot. "Hi there, Mr. Forbes."

Mr. Forbes, one of the developers of Cypress, shook his head at her but she saw the hint of a smile beneath his salt-and-pepper moustache. "You were saying, Tammy? Something about tonight's outing?"

Tammy sat up a little bit straighter. Wearing her usual work clothes of a silk blouse and crisp linen skirt, she knew she projected a professional image. Her hair was still straight and neat too, despite the breeze she'd kicked up on the golf cart with her last tour. It all felt like a costume at the moment, however.

She held on to the cool reserve she fought to maintain at all times and gave him a smooth smile. "I was just telling Oliver that you can count on me, sir."

He gave a nod. "Good. You're our best salesperson, no

offense to Oliver here, and I need you to mingle with the prospective residents we've invited. You remember the invitations going out, don't you my dear?"

She nodded. Boy, did she. The staff had worked their fingers to the bone emailing practically every family who'd ever taken a tour of Cypress over the past six months.

"Of course, Mr. Forbes."

"Rick is counting on you to be there," he continued. "You wouldn't want to disappoint him, would you?"

Jeez, way to pile it on. Rick Chapman was the Sales Director and she counted him as a friend as well as her boss. He was good for Cypress and she knew just what that meant to the bottom line. And to her own commission earnings.

"Never, sir." She saw Ollie smirking from where he leaned against the wall. "Oliver and I will be there with bells on."

Ollie's blue eyes rounded and his perfect angel face went a little pale. "It should be a blast," he croaked.

Mr. Forbes gave another brisk nod and left her office. Ollie shut the door and sat on the corner of her desk.

"Thanks for that," he said.

"Shut up," she said without anger. "Now we have to go play the family stuff tonight. Great. So much for the beach."

"How do you think I feel?" Ollie asked. "It's not exactly my scene, you know."

Tammy leveled a gaze at him. "Your people can marry now, Ollie. Shouldn't you be hooking up with your forever love and adopting a couple of boxers?"

"French bulldogs, and not yet thanks." He waved a hand. "What about you? Your best friend is married to that daredevil, Jake Chapman. And blazing-hot nature boy Ty is going to marry Jake's little sister in two weeks. When's your turn?"

"My turn for what?"

"Family stuff, Tammy. For real."

She gave a dramatic shiver. "None for me, thanks. All my family is up in Jersey, happily populating the Shore as we speak."

Ollie grinned. "How many nieces and nephews is it now?"

Tammy groaned. "Jeez, I've lost count. I have three sisters and two brothers, all married and having babies left and right. My family procreates like it's 1945 and the Allies just liberated Europe."

Ollie laughed out loud. "You're bad."

"I'm serious." She blew out a breath and leaned back in her chair once more. "I'm glad, in a way. It keeps my mother off my

15

back about doing the family thing any time soon. That's a good thing, since I'm twenty-seven and by that age she already had three kids herself."

Ollie shook his head. "But what about the romance thing?"

Tammy nibbled her bottom lip. She'd had little crushes on just about every hot guy who'd come to work at Cypress, and flirted hard with them too. She'd never pushed it past flirting, though. It seemed to her that they all fell fast for their own true loves. And once a guy showed serious interest in another girl? It was hands off where she was concerned.

First there had been Rick Chapman, who'd fallen hard for Harmony from the Cypress Institute. Then his brother Jake, who Tammy had to admit was an extra-delicious slice of pie. And she couldn't forget Ty Walsh, the wild-animal tamer who was well and caught by the only Chapman girl, Cassie. Amazingly, they all seemed so happy.

Seeing her own siblings, sweethearts all and apparently truly in love with their spouses, convinced her that you couldn't have commitment without consequences. She shivered as she thought about juggling carpool, strollers and soccer dates. Fall in love, lose yourself. And your freedom.

Tammy hadn't wanted anything real with Rick, Jake or Ty,

16

though. Flirting was just part of her DNA. It was harmless and actually helped her in her chosen career. She had charm in spades, her father always told her. Now, at Cypress, she could work that charm to her advantage. And keep her heart completely out of it.

"Romance?" she asked. "Not my thing."

Another knock came at the door and Ollie opened it. Rick stood there, an expectant look on his face.

"Hey, Rick," she said.

"Hey. Good, you're both in here."

Tammy and Ollie both stood.

"What's up?" Ollie asked.

"I want you guys to meet my brother."

Tammy laughed a little. "Okay. I believe we know Jake pretty well by now."

Rick smiled. "No. My half-brother, Ben. He came down for a short visit a few weeks ago, but I didn't get a chance to introduce you to him."

Rick stepped back and Ollie was the first out the door. He stood still as he caught a glimpse of who was just outside her field of vision. Rick's half-brother, she presumed. Then Ollie slid a glance at Tammy from beneath raised eyebrows.

"Ben, this is Oliver Wright and Tammy Donato," Rick said. "Tammy. Ollie. My brother, Ben Chapman."

With a smile fixed on her face, Tammy stepped into the hall to join them. Then she got a look at Rick's brother and her stomach tumbled down to her toes.

"Hi." Rick's brother's voice was deep and a little bit husky. "Nice to meet you."

Ollie said something in return but Tammy just stared dumbly at Ben Chapman. He was tall and looked strong. His jeans were a little worn and they hung off his narrow hips just right. The pale green polo he wore looked soft stretched across his broad chest. As she brought her gaze higher she saw that this guy had Rick's chiseled good looks and Jake's cocky grin, and a dusting of stubble darkened his cheeks for good measure. His eyes were a blue-gray and his thick, dark hair was tousled.

He stared back at her and she finally realized that she still hadn't said a darn thing.

"N-nice to meet you," she said at last.

His eyes flicked to Ollie and back to her. "Rick said you're just the one to give me a tour of the place, Tammy."

She nodded but couldn't seem to speak. What the hell was wrong with her?

"Sure thing." She finally said, sounding like an idiot. "Anything you want. I mean, any time you want."

Ben flashed a smile and she felt the heat of it all over her skin. "Great."

Chapter 2

"I'll leave you two to make the arrangements." Ben's brother Rick clapped the blond guy on the shoulder. "Ollie, I wanted to ask you about that tour you did yesterday. The corporate guys from Tampa?"

The blond guy nodded and followed Rick down toward what Ben guessed was the director's office, leaving him alone with Miss Tammy Donato.

She looked very cool and collected. She was dressed primly but a couple of strategic buttons were undone on her pretty pink shirt. She had all the right curves under that simple tan skirt, too. She was a little bit taller than his brother's wives and those heels brought her almost up to his shoulder.

"Tammy, huh?"

She nodded, her full rosy lips curved upward at one corner. "Tamara, actually. Accent on the 'ma.'"

"Tamara."

Her hazel eyes sparkled. He'd even rolled the r just a little, like she had.

"Yeah. It's Italian." She leaned against the wall and crossed her ankles. "So, Ben Chapman. Are you going to the event tonight?"

"The picnic?" At her nod he shrugged a shoulder. "Harmony insisted and I find I can't say no to her."

"She's a force of nature. A gentle, insistent wind in your ear."

Ben smiled again. He'd been down in Cypress for just a day now, but he had to agree with Tammy's assessment. On his last visit he hadn't had a chance to do more than a quick meet-and-greet with his newfound family and in-laws. Maybe this time he'd get to know them all a little bit better.

"Will you be there?" he asked.

She leaned closer and tilted her head, causing her dark shining hair to slide over one shoulder. He could smell her now. Her scent was something like flowers and spice. *Mmm.*

"I was commanded to, so I guess I have to," she said with a wide smile.

Her smile was amazing, too. A little bit crooked, which quirked her lips up another notch. Her skin had a soft hint of olive to it and look as smooth as silk.

"Then I guess I'll see you there," he said.

Those golden-green eyes of hers flicked over him, nice and slow. "Oh, you'll see me."

21

Ben felt a flash of heat straight down to his groin. *Whoa.* He might be new to Cypress but he wasn't some dumb kid from Cali. He knew flirting when he saw it and sweet Tamara Donato was definitely flirting with him.

"Good." It was his turn to run his own gaze slowly over her toned curves. "I look forward to seeing more of you."

Her eyes widened and she gave a little shiver. It was clear the girl was used to turning it on but never really got it in return. Ben hid his smile. He could give as good as he got, or so his last few hook-ups had attested. Not that he'd hooked up much in the past year.

"Until then." She turned and he was treated to the sweet view of her ass as she walked back into her office.

Ben stood there, his body tingling. Yeah she was pretty, but he'd seen plenty of beauties growing up in Santa Cruz. The beachside town was wall-to-wall hard bodies. But there was something about this girl.

She wasn't as smooth and cool as she put on. He'd seen the flicker of awareness in her gaze when they'd been alone. And when he'd flirted back? She'd trembled.

He gave himself a mental shake and turned away from her door. He was here to get to know his family. That was all. To be a part of his little sister's wedding, as mind-blowing as that was to comprehend. As to his father's demands? Bill could take a leap off of one of Jake's rope bridges if he believed for one second that Ben would spy for him.

He headed to the breakroom Rick had pointed out earlier to grab a bottle of water. There was a guy in the room, a man about his father's age. Ben lifted his chin in greeting.

"Ben, is it?" the guy asked.

"Yes. Rick's brother." That still felt strange to say. "Ben Chapman."

"Paul Forbes, Ben." Forbes held his hand out. "One of the developers of Cypress."

Ben shook his hand. "Very nice to meet you, Mr. Forbes."

The man crossed his arms over his chest. He was a solid guy with graying hair and a trim mustache. His dark eyes sparkled and Ben guessed this guy was always thinking.

"So, another Chapman. How did I get so lucky?"

Ben smiled. "I don't know about luck."

Forbes sat at one of the tables and waved his hand at the chair opposite. Ben took the seat and folded his hands on the table.

"What can I do for you, Mr. Forbes?"

23

"I heard you're an architect."

Ben kept his expression even. "Yes."

"Then you have to help us with our new green, eco-friendly homes."

"I'm assuming you've already got a team in place, Mr. Forbes."

Forbes gave a quick nod. "We do. But we need some fresh blood. The builders down here have their way of doing things, you know."

"And from what my brother Rick tells me, they've brought a lot of success to Cypress with their designs."

"Yes, the classic home styles are very popular."

"And timeless. I've driven through a few of the villages. The homes are pretty and the settings welcoming."

"Thank you for saying so, Ben. But these builders aren't comfortable with some of the features in the energy-wise homes we're planning. I'm assuming by working out in California you're experienced with the new developments?"

"Sure. Air quality is a big deal out there. The state is very forward-thinking when it comes to conservation and energy savings, not to mention the impact on the environment."

Forbes smiled. "I knew you'd be the perfect guy for this."

Ben studied Forbes and he didn't seem to have a hidden agenda. No. Cypress Corners was his baby and he wanted only the best people working in it. Ben had enough confidence left to realize he could be one of the best. Even if he hadn't been able to design a damn thing in months.

"What, precisely, would my input be?" he asked Forbes.

"I want you to design homes implementing the best new energy-saving technologies. Along with the state-of-the-art features we already have in place for convenience and communication. Oh, and keeping the homes classic in style."

Ben arched his brows. "Is that all?"

Forbes laughed softly. "Let's just say you would have a lot on your plate but your father said you're up to the challenge."

"You spoke to my father about me?"

"He called me, yes. I took the liberty of looking into your credentials and awards. Very impressive, I must say." He winked. "I shouldn't be surprised, though. Both of your brothers are the best at what they do, too."

Ben found he kind of liked being compared to his brothers that way. It was true he'd enjoyed a lot of success back in California. He was proud of his awards and prouder still of the homes he'd built for his clients.

"What are you asking of me, Mr. Forbes?"

Forbes shook his head. "This isn't the place to discuss this, Ben. Why don't you come by my office Monday morning? Let's say nine o'clock."

Ben's mind worked around the man's words. Did he want to talk about a job here in Cypress? There was a lot to consider. Hey, he wouldn't have to go back to Boston. The busy work his father handed him was just not enough to float his boat. He could certainly use some direction in his life at this point, too. He'd been stagnating in Santa Cruz since his mother got sick. Plus he missed the spark of creativity that used to drive him. Maybe if he worked on the green homes he could find that thrill again.

"I'd be happy to meet with you on Monday, sir. Thanks so much for considering me."

"Thank you, Ben. I know there's a lot to take in, seeing that you're new to Cypress and all." He snapped his fingers. "I tell you what. Why don't you schedule a tour with Tammy for Monday as well? She's our best, believe me."

Ben's lips twitched. He doubted the man had the slightest idea of the images his words put in Ben's mind.

"I look forward to it."

Forbes stood. "See you tonight at the picnic?"

Again, Ben thought about Tammy. He grinned. "I wouldn't miss it."

***

"I can't believe you actually came."

Tammy snorted and looked at her best friend, Claire Chapman. The CPA money mind of Cypress, Claire was precise and perfect and Tammy didn't know what she would do without her friendship.

"Mr. Forbes insisted." Tammy sipped at her mason jar of lemonade. "Believe me, you couldn't drag me to one of these family things otherwise."

Claire waved a hand and flicked her strawberry-blond waves over her shoulder. "Jake said the same thing but he knows I like these outings."

Tammy studied her friend. She knew that Claire and her husband were trying to get pregnant, but every month Claire wore an expression of sad resignation and determination Tammy couldn't miss.

When Claire's gaze ran over the guests and Cypress employees populating the main lakeshore, she could easily see the yearning in her eyes. Tammy followed her line of vision and saw that Rick and Harmony were running around the playground with their little son, Nick.

Tammy tilted her head. She had to admit, the kid was a looker. And not annoying in the least. If Claire and Jake had a baby, there was every possibility they would be just as blessed. The thought caught her off guard. Blessed? Since when did she ever think such a thing when considering the plague of babies her family inflicted on the world?

"It'll happen," Tammy said in a low voice.

"Hmm?" Claire tucked a strand of hair behind her ear. "I know, I know. Jake says the same thing."

Tammy nudged her with her elbow. "And how much fun is the trying, huh?"

Claire's creamy complexion showed pink and Tammy laughed.

"You're so easy," Tammy said.

"Stop embarrassing me, then," Claire said.

"Nope." Tammy took another sip of lemonade. "Jeez, do they ever have anything stronger at these things?"

"No. This isn't happy hour."

"It sure isn't happy for me."

Claire clicked her tongue. "Ollie seems to be making the

most of it."

Tammy looked over to find Ollie holding court with a few of the families he'd toured most recently.

"The boy can sell."

"That's because he isn't buying," Claire said. "He's worse than you."

"Worse than me?" Tammy blinked. "What does that mean?"

Claire's eyes sparkled. "Nothing. I just mean that you enjoy your single lifestyle."

"Why shouldn't I? You know, we've had this conversation before. I'm in no hurry to join the ranks. Believe me."

"Oh, I believe you. I just don't believe you're as happy as you let on."

Tammy scoffed. "Believe what you want, girl. My time is my own."

Claire nodded idly, her eyes still on Nick and the other kids running roughshod over the playground equipment.

Just then, Mr. Forbes came into Tammy's field of vision. He waved to her and she lifted her mason jar in silent salute. He just continued to wave, now beckoning her over to where he stood under one of the canopies Cypress had installed for the event.

"This evening gets better and better," she said. "Mr. Forbes probably wants me to push the kids on the swing."

Claire laughed. "Go."

Tammy smirked at her, and then walked over to the developer. "Hello, Mr. Forbes."

"Tammy." He sounded very satisfied. "You came."

"I was expressly urged to do so," she said.

He chuckled. "That's very true. Is it as frightening as you envisioned?"

"I'll survive." She smiled. "Seriously, you know I'm all about Cypress. If I have to endure—I'm sorry, *enjoy*—a few of these events once in a while, I figure that comes with the territory."

"That's a smart attitude." The man's sharp gaze focused on the fringe of the playground. "There's someone I want you to meet."

"Who?"

"Ben!" he called.

Tammy's heart tripped as she turned to see Ben Chapman headed their way.

"So glad you could make it," Forbes said, shaking Ben's hand in greeting. "Have you met Tammy?"

Ben turned those blue-gray eyes in her direction. "I have,

30

yes. This afternoon. Hello again, Tamara."

"Tammy," she corrected him. "Tammy is fine."

Forbes looked between the both of them, but she guessed he missed the heat sparking between her and Ben.

"Good, good. I want Tammy to take you on a tour Monday. After our meeting."

Ben nodded. "That would be great."

Tammy just studied his strong throat as she tried to slow her pulse. What was it about this guy? She loved the way he said her name, though. Yeah, he was smoking hot but he was connected to too many other people in her life. She anticipated messiness if they got involved. And she so did not do messy.

"I'll leave you kids to sort out the details," Mr. Forbes said.

And with that, the guy left her and Ben relatively alone.

"So, this isn't really your thing," Ben said.

Tammy shrugged. "I'm here, aren't I?"

He met her gaze dead on. "Are you?"

"What are you getting at?"

"You just don't seem like the home and hearth type."

She sucked in a breath, supremely irritated. "You don't even know me."

"Are you saying you're eager to add to the population of

this pretty little town?"

She pulled her eyes away from his. "I'm not saying anything of the kind. I'm here at the developer's urging. That's all."

Ben shoved his hands in the front pockets of his jeans. The action served to pull them down just enough to show her a sliver of lighter skin above the waistband.

"This isn't my scene, either," he said.

"But you have family here."

He was quiet for a second, his brows drawn a little closer together. "Yeah. Family."

Tammy didn't know much about how Ben figured into the picture, but she'd never heard the guy mentioned before last spring. He clearly belonged to the Chapmans, though. In looks and mannerisms, at least.

"My family is all up north, thank God," she said.

"Oh? Where?"

"South Jersey."

"Do you get home much?"

"Not if I can help it." When Ben's brows arched, she shook her head with a laugh. "Don't get me wrong. I love my family. They're just a lot to take. Lots of brothers and sisters and too many nieces and nephews to count. Believe me, the Donato family is large and in charge."

Ben nodded. "I have no idea what that's like. I thought I was an only child for twenty-eight years."

She wanted to ask him just what happened to drop him into the bosom of his newfound family, but it really wasn't her business.

"You're very lucky to have Rick, Jake and Cassie as family."

"Yeah." His voice still had that flat tone. "They seem nice."

"They are. You'll fit right in."

He looked at her in apparent surprise. "What makes you think I want to fit in?"

Tammy thought about his question for a minute. It was clear he was looking for something. And like he had no idea what that something was. She couldn't say that to him, though.

"I just figured you would want to get to know them all better," she said.

"I do."

"Your sister Cassie's wedding should be a great opportunity for that. The day's, what? Two weeks from tomorrow?"

He rolled his eyes but a smile teased his full mouth. A dimple showed on one cheek. "That's what she tells me."

Tammy smiled back. "Then there you go. There's nothing like a wedding to bring a family together."

"You've gone to a lot of them, I take it?"

She held up a hand with all her fingers splayed. "Hey, three sisters and two brothers. All married in true Italian fashion. Huge church wedding with a ton of attendants. A venetian table of desserts and too many meal courses to count. The Tarantella, the Chicken Dance. Believe me, I'm looking forward to a nice, normal ceremony with a nice normal party to follow."

Ben chuckled. "I bet they'll still play the Chicken Dance."

Tammy laughed and placed her hand on his arm. "If that's the worst of it, I'm in."

He stilled and she felt his forearm tense beneath her fingers. "It'll be a first for me. A family wedding."

Before she could say something more they were joined by Rick and Harmony. Harmony was a natural beauty, with clear hazel eyes and honey-colored curls she usually pulled up into a ponytail.

"Hi there, Tammy," Harmony said with a smile.

"Hi, Harmony." She pulled her hand away from Ben's arm. "Rick."

Harmony turned to Ben. "Having a good time, Ben?"

"Sure."

Harmony looked back at Tammy. "I know you always head to the beach on the weekends, but if you're around on Sunday we'd love it if you stopped by the house."

Tammy quirked her lips. "One of Rick's famous barbeque picnics, I take it?"

Harmony nodded. "With Claire bringing the treats, of course."

Tammy grinned and looked over at Ben. "Claire is the world's best, most precise baker, Ben. If you haven't heard that already."

"I haven't, no," Ben said.

"Her chocolate-chocolate chip cookies are to die for," Harmony said.

"Then you'll have to come," Ben said to Tammy.

Her heart flipped for a different reason. She'd managed to avoid those Sunday picnics for years now. Even the lure of Claire's cookies couldn't drag her from her weekly beach escape.

"I don't think so," she managed to say.

Did Ben look a little disappointed? That wouldn't last long. He'd get to know his family. His little nephew. Maybe even realize that family was just what he wanted. That settling down was just what he needed.

And that so made him not the guy she needed.

Chapter 3

Sunday morning, Ben sat in the dining room of the Cypress Inn. Although he'd stayed with Rick and Harmony when he'd last visited, he hadn't wanted to impose again. The bed and breakfast was really quite comfortable. It was designed to look like a stately Victorian but Ben knew it had only been built about five years ago.

Three stories tall, the B and B sat on a rise not far from the main lakeshore. It was designed well, which he could appreciate. And situated in a near-perfect setting. If it had been his project he would have included more period details, though. When you took the sweeping staircase up to the hallway leading to the guest rooms, that was where the illusion dimmed a little bit.

A huge wraparound porch and wide balconies off of several of the fifteen guest rooms took advantage of the view. He could just see the sun glinting off the ripples in the lake through the open French doors of the dining room. It wasn't the Pacific Ocean, but the gentle pull of the water spoke to him just the same.

"More coffee, Mr. Chapman?" the innkeeper asked.

Ben smiled at the elderly woman. "No, thanks. I'm good."

She smiled, folding her hands over her midsection. "Then you must have another cinnamon roll. They don't sell these at the bakery in the town center, you know."

"An exclusive?" he teased. "They're delicious. That's quite a coup."

"I know!" She beamed at him, patting her graying hair back from her brow. "I can't touch the drinks from the coffee shop, though."

"And they can't touch the ambiance here at the Cypress Inn."

The woman blushed and hurried over to the sideboard to grab him another of their exclusive cinnamon rolls. Ben waved it away with a smile and downed the remains of his cup of coffee.

He wasn't expected at Rick and Harmony's until around one, so he figured he'd head out to the lake and do some thinking. The dining room was getting a little crowded now that it was coming up on ten o'clock. He wasn't in the mood for more small talk and he needed peace and quiet to figure out just what he was going to tell Mr. Forbes tomorrow morning. At the moment, he had no idea.

After thanking the innkeeper again, he headed out the French doors to the terrace and took the steps down to the inn's secluded portion of the lakeshore beach. It was a warm morning and, from the last couple of days spent here, he knew it would get pretty hot later. Harmony had told him that summer wouldn't begin to release its hold on Central Florida until October. Would he still be here in October? If he took the job Forbes offered, yeah he would.

He reached the soft, sandy path and stood there for a second. The lakeshore was unlike anything he'd seen in California. Towering oaks and cypress trees dripping with Spanish moss framed the incredible views of the crystal blue lake. He could hear kids' laughter and the ebb and flow of voices from the more-populated main lakeshore somewhere to his right but here, at the base of the inn, it was pretty quiet. Almost serene.

A row of lounge chairs stretched out in front of him, all turned to face the lake view. They were all unoccupied too, except for one. As he drew closer he caught a glimpse of long, tanned legs. Intrigued, he continued as the rest of the sunbather came into view. Those shapely legs drew his eyes up and over a flat bare belly to round, full breasts barely contained in a hot pink bikini top. Oversized sunglasses covered half of the woman's face but he'd know that silky dark hair anywhere. It was Tammy Donato herself.

He stood in front of her, letting his shadow play over her face. When she let out a breath, he almost felt it brush over his body.

"Good morning," he said.

She started, and then peeked at him over her sunglasses. A slow smile curved her lips as she leaned up on her elbows. "Well, well. If it isn't the newest Chapman in town."

"Yep." He chuckled and sat down on the lounge beside hers. "I'm staying up at the inn. What's your excuse?"

She shrugged, and then slid her sunglasses up on her head. "Mr. Forbes roped me into that picnic Friday, you know. I had to get my beach time in somehow."

"Why not head to the main lakeshore?"

She gave a shudder. "Too many kids, thanks." She winked at him. "You're not going to rat me out, are you?"

He shook his head. "Nope. I'm with you on the peace and quiet thing." He dragged his eyes from the hot-as-hell picture she made on her lounger and looked toward the lake again. "I have some thinking to do."

She sat up and swung her legs to one side of the lounge chair. "About what?" She held up one hand. "I'm not prying, I swear. Despite what Harmony and Claire say, I'm no Lettie."

He brought his attention back to her. "Who's Lettie?"

Tammy slanted him a look. "You haven't met Lettie yet? Oh, just wait." Her eyes ran over him. "She's going to just love you."

"What?"

"Don't worry. She's harmless. She's 'a woman of a certain age' but there's still fire in her furnace. Or something like that. She's just full of those Southern sayings. Talking with her is like watching *Steel Magnolias*."

He dipped his head. "I look forward to making her acquaintance, then," he drawled.

She laughed. "Yep. That accent was awful but she's going to eat you up with a spoon anyway."

The words were innocent but with her wearing next to nothing his mind went straight to where it shouldn't. Shifting on the lounger, he rested his arms on his knees and clasped his hands. She leaned on one elbow now, her hair sliding over her shoulder to graze her incredible body.

"So what's got you doing the deep thinking this morning, Ben?"

"Mr. Forbes wants me to meet with him tomorrow."

"And to take a tour with me afterwards."

"Yeah." He blew out a breath. "I think he wants to offer me a job."

She blinked at him. "What kind of job? In sales?"

"No." He grinned at her. "What, are you worried I'll take your place as the best salesperson at Cypress?"

She snorted. "Not likely."

He laughed a little. "He wants me to do some design work."

"You're a designer?"

He swallowed, his eyes going to the lake view again. "An architect, actually."

"Hmm."

He looked at her again. "What?"

"You know we have a new village going in. With homes so green you can almost eat the walls."

"And?"

"Forbes must want a fresh eye, so to speak."

His stomach churned. "That's what I'm afraid of."

***

Tammy straightened as she read the bemusement on Ben's face. Something was up with this guy. That was for sure.

"What's the problem?" she asked.

He flashed her a smile again, that dimple playing hide and

seek. He looked good. He was dressed more casually today, with a weathered blue t-shirt, tan cargo shorts and sneakers. His long legs were braced apart and his strong-looking hands were still clasped.

"Problem?" He ran a hand through those dark tousled waves of his. "No problem, really. I just…" He shook his head and fixed his eyes on her. "It's a beautiful Sunday morning, Tammy. I'm sitting here on a serene beach with a gorgeous girl. Nope. No problem at all."

She felt that heat from him, like she had yesterday. He wasn't exactly flirting but the impact was the same. This guy was dangerous. He had sex appeal in every inch of his fit body and she could hardly catch her breath.

"No problem at all?" She shrugged. "Must be nice."

He laughed, low and soft. "Very nice."

Oh! She had to put some space between them before she jumped him right here in full view of the inn's guests and the families playing just down the other end of the beach.

Forcing herself to look cool and calm even as her heart was hammering in her chest, she lowered herself back down on the lounger. Sunglasses in place and hiding her from him once more, she could breathe a little easier.

"You're welcome to stretch out and do your thinking right here," she said. "Problem or no problem."

He was quiet, so she peeked over at him. He was studying his hands, running them over his thighs. His brow was knit and his lips pressed together. He had a problem. No matter what he might say otherwise.

"No, I think I'll leave you to your beach," he finally said.

"It's not my beach. I'm an intruder."

"I'll just tell the innkeeper that you're my guest."

She propped herself up on her elbows again. "Your guest?"

He dipped his head but she caught his smile. "Maybe you can drop by sometime."

She sat up. "What are you asking me, Ben?"

He splayed a hand over his chest. "Hey, I just thought you might want to join me for breakfast one morning."

"Breakfast, huh?"

"My mother raised me to be a gentleman, Tamara. I'd never send a girl home hungry."

Her mouth dropped open. Was he seriously propositioning her? In an instant, the impression of rolling around with Ben on a big bed in one of the inn's guest rooms made her pulse race.

She managed an easy smile even as she flushed hotter than

the sun in the cloudless sky. "I think you've got your signals crossed, pal."

"If you say so." He chuckled, the sound sliding over her just right. "So will I see you at Rick and Harmony's?"

"All that family stuff? Um, I don't think so."

"All that family is right. You said you have tons of brothers and sisters. Maybe you can help me figure out how to act around so many family members."

"Nuh-uh. My family's up north, remember?"

"It would be nice to have a friend there," he said.

Now she rose a little more to sit cross-legged. The sunglasses slid up on top of her head again so she could face him fully. "So, we're friends now?"

One brow arched. "Aren't we?"

"You've known me all of thirty-six hours, Ben. And since we spoke a total of fifteen minutes on Friday, I'd say we're not exactly at the 'hey, I got your back' or 'bro, do me a solid' point in our relationship."

"Maybe not." His eyes dipped down to her chest and back to her eyes. "Would it help if I told you I thought about you last night? In the shower?"

"Ben!" She saw the sparkle in his eyes then and shook her

head. "You're a little naughty, you know that?"

"So you'll come today?"

She picked up her towel off the back of the lounger and dabbed her face. He could really make her sweat.

Lowering the towel, she faced him again. "Oh, okay."

The smile that spread across his face took her breath.

"Great," he said. "It's at one."

She waved a hand. "I know what time it is, believe me. I've been dodging these things for years now."

He stood, looking very tall standing there so close to her. "Good. I'll leave you to a little bit of peace then. I'll see you at...my brother's."

With that, he left her and she gave up on any uncluttered musings for the rest of the morning. She was going to Rick and Harmony's this afternoon, as amazing as that should be. And she was going as Ben's friend. *Jeez.*

At one fifteen she stood on the porch of Rick and Harmony's house with one arm wrapped around a potted bromeliad plant. It was pretty but what Tammy knew about plants would just about fit in the glossy blue pot that held this one. Thank God she'd been able to find Lettie at home today. After despairing of ever getting back to her contemplative state she'd achieved before handsome Ben Chapman had intruded on her stolen solitude, that was. Lettie, the sweet and outrageous fixture of Cypress Corners with a greener thumb than even Harmony, was only too happy to recommend the perfect houseplant.

Rick and Harmony's house was a gorgeous two-story and Tammy knew it inside and out, but not from frequent visits. No. She was well-versed in all of the construction in the different villages and this particular house was situated in one of the more spacious of them. The large lot and all of the high-end fixtures should have made the house look grand and off-putting but this home was very welcoming.

It claimed a beautiful view of the central lakeshore across the street, and a deep porch stretched across the front. Adirondack chairs and a hanging bench swing beckoned visitors to the porch enclosed by columns and a railing. The house was painted a dove gray and the roof was peaked slate.

Rick had chosen well when he picked this property. And when he'd chosen his wife. She knew it was Harmony's touch that made this home so...homey. If Tammy had been taxed with that duty, there was no telling what the place would look and feel like.

Taking a breath, she rapped on the wooden screen door. The front door opened with a whoosh and she looked down to see Nick Chapman blinking up at her.

"Tammy!"

The kid's enthusiasm took her by surprise. She'd known the boy since he was a bump on Harmony's trim body but she didn't think he really paid her much attention. Huh. Who knew?

"Hey there, Nick."

He grinned now. "Mommy was sure you were coming but Daddy said no way."

She laughed. "Hmm. Do you want to be the one to give them the news?"

Nick bobbed his head and turned away from the door. "Mommy, you were right!"

His voice trailed behind him as he ran toward the back of the house. Tammy shifted from foot to foot, and then reached for the door handle.

"Let me get that."

She stiffened as Ben's voice reached her. He seemed to materialize out of the shadows through the screening and then he was there, pushing the door open and beckoning her inside. He wore sneakers and cargo shorts again, now paired with a light blue polo. He looked really good and she stopped herself from drooling.

"Thanks," she managed to say.

"Thanks for coming." His gaze ran over her, from her strappy wedges up over her bare legs to her khaki shorts. Her body tingled as he eyed her soft Henley t-shirt before settling on her face again. "You look good."

Not "nice." "Good." She liked the way he said that, too. Simple, yet really hot. She couldn't forget his backhanded proposition of that morning, either. Was he serious? Did she want him to be?

God, she didn't know. She sidestepped him and headed for the kitchen. One good thing about never thinking about forever?

She didn't have to make her mind up about it right now.

Chapter 4

Harmony met her in the kitchen with a big smile. "Tammy, you came." She winked. "Rick owes me ten bucks."

Tammy smiled. "Happy to help." She held out the plant. "This is for you."

Harmony took the plant, her eyes wide. "Oh, what a gorgeous *vriesea splendens*! That's a flaming sword."

"Okay," Tammy said with a chuckle.

"A what?" Ben asked from behind her.

Tammy managed to keep from jumping. How did such a big guy move so quietly?

She threw him a glance over her shoulder. "Harmony's a botany brain, Ben."

"Yep." Harmony placed the plant on the raised granite counter, turning the pot until it faced whatever way she believed it should, and faced Tammy again. "It's lovely. Thank you."

"Thanks for inviting me," Tammy said. "Again."

Harmony flashed her another smile. Rick came up behind Harmony and dropped a kiss on her cheek.

"That's pretty," he said with a nod to the plant. "Ben, come man the grill a minute? I have to grab the cheese and stuff.

50

Harmony says I made the burgers too thick, but you tell me."

"Too thick?" Ben shook his head. "That's not possible."

"Right?" Rick patted Tammy on the shoulder. "Nice to see you here, Tammy."

"Even if it cost you ten bucks?" Tammy teased.

Rick shrugged and grabbed a plate stacked with cheese slices out of the wide stainless fridge. "Come on, Ben. If Jake has his way, he'll take the burgers off while they're still mooing."

Ben followed his big brother thought the French doors onto the patio. She didn't miss how Ben carried himself, though. He still appeared a little bit uncomfortable around these people.

"Hmm," she mused aloud.

"What's that?" Harmony asked.

Tammy started, and then faced Harmony. "What's what?"

"You look like you're thinking about something, and it can't just be my new brother-in-law's very fine butt."

Tammy gaped at her. "Harmony!" She quickly saw through the French doors that Nick was out on the patio with Claire and Jake, which explained Harmony's easy comment. "He does have a fine butt, but I was wondering about just how long he's been in the family. It seems really new."

"It is." Harmony poured them each a glass of lemonade and settled on one of the tall barstools. "Bill broke the news to them last spring. When Cassie first came down here."

"What happened when I came down here?" Cassie Chapman breezed into the kitchen from the direction of the front door. "I caused a major disturbance in the force, right Ty?"

Cassie's fiancé, Ty Walsh, followed behind. He carried a bottle of wine and a six-pack of beer bottles, which he placed beside Tammy's plant.

Tammy smiled at her newest Cypress friend. Cassie was the youngest Chapman. She had the gorgeous looks of her brothers, with long dark hair and big blue eyes. She'd come down here without any direction last spring and now she had a place and a guy who loved her. A pang of want settled in Tammy's belly. What was wrong with her today? She didn't lust after Cassie's guy, and she sure as hell didn't lust after what Cassie had.

"Harmony was just telling me about how you found out about Ben," Tammy said.

Cassie's mouth, always ready to smile, thinned to a line. "Our father, that paragon of men, announced it casually over dinner."

Ty's hazel eyes grew clouded as he placed a hand on

Cassie's shoulder. "Easy," he drawled.

His touch seemed to soothe her, which wasn't surprising since he was the wild animal tamer of Cypress. Cassie covered Ty's hand with hers and leaned back against him, letting out a breath. "Sorry. Talking about Bill always gets me upset."

"Have you decided if he's coming to the wedding?" Harmony asked.

Cassie gave a quick shake of her head. "Nope. No decision yet."

"Tick tock," Tammy put in.

"Yeah, I know," Cassie said. "But I figure I can wait until the last minute, since he has absolutely nothing to do with the planning."

Ty kissed her neck, drawing a soft laugh out of her, and stepped back. "Let me go say hello to the guys."

"Yeah, yeah," Harmony said, waving a hand. "You just want to cook meat over fire, like the rest of them."

Ty grinned, and then went out onto the patio.

"So, Tammy." Cassie leaned an elbow on the tall counter. "We're finally blessed with your presence."

Tammy's cheeks heated a little, and she fingered the hem of her t-shirt. "I was roped into the picnic Friday night, so I was around this weekend."

Cassie stared at her for a beat, her eyes wide. "You went to that picnic? Seriously?"

"Jeez, it's not like I'm antisocial," Tammy said.

"No." Cassie's eyes sparkled. "But you're not exactly a *family*-social kind of girl."

"True," Tammy admitted. "But that doesn't mean I can't tow the company line."

"What is this, a middle-school dance?" Claire Chapman said as she stepped in from the patio.

"Hey." Tammy waved to her best friend. "I prefer 'hen party,' actually."

"Boys and girls, separated." Claire hugged Cassie hello, and then placed her arm around Tammy's shoulders. "Good to see you here."

Tammy felt herself ease. Claire looked bright and pretty today, with her strawberry hair pulled back in a low ponytail. Her skin looked flushed, and Tammy guessed she'd just been manhandled by her husband.

"Jake and the guys ruling the roost out there?" Harmony asked.

"Yep." Claire walked over to the fridge. "Let me grab the

salad and we can start this shindig."

With that, they seemed to move as one. Tammy stood there, feeling lost as the three of them worked like a well-oiled machine. With her family, in her mother's overcrowded kitchen, there seemed to be ordered chaos. They all worked together there, too. Except for Tammy. She'd always managed to keep out of the fray.

"Coming?" Cassie asked, a brow raised as she waved a stack of napkins at her.

Tammy mentally shook herself. "Sure."

She followed them out onto the patio, her feet moving slowly as she braced herself for more family stuff.

***

Ben stood facing the grill, his legs braced as he twirled the long-handled spatula in one hand. He'd lost some of his unease, probably because he was given a job to do. He had to hand it to his big brother. Rick knew people. That was for sure.

"Those burgers ready yet?" Jake called from his seat at the big picnic table. "You're not overcooking them, are you bro?"

Ben smiled as he threw Jake a look over his shoulder. "Keeping them juicy, man. I promise."

"Good." Jake grinned at him. "I like it pink." He grabbed his wife in a hug. "Like my women."

Claire blushed to the roots of her pretty red hair, which had clearly been what Jake had intended. Ben glanced over to the French doors where his little sister was waving hello at him. He lifted his chin in greeting, and then stilled when he saw that Tammy followed behind. *Damn.* The girl really was smoking hot today.

Sure, she wore a t-shirt and shorts but he knew what was underneath those casual clothes. Yeah, he'd gotten a good look this morning at the lakeshore. No shame in it.

She stared back at him, her eyes sparkling. Was she thinking about his proposition, too? He'd only been half-kidding. He might not have known her for more than a couple of days but he knew he wanted her in that nice, big bed in his room at the inn. It was complicated, though. When he thought she was friendly with his family, it had been in an abstract kind of way. Today, though? Today she was in the thick of it.

After they stared at each other for a long heated minute, Tammy joined the others at the table. Rick and Nick joined the others, and the little boy looked as hungry as the rest of them. Carnivores. Hey, he might be from greens-and-seeds country but he liked cow, too. It was yet another point where he felt a connection. He turned back to the grill.

"Okay, who wants cheese?" he asked.

Rick came over and threw slices of cheese on about half of the burgers, and then handed Ben a platter. "Plate those up, Ben?"

Ben nodded and soon lunch was served. He sat down across from Tammy, sharing a smile that he saw Harmony didn't miss. He looked away. He couldn't help it if every time he looked at Tammy he pictured her in that skimpy bathing suit, could he? The sun kissing all that smooth skin, touching on the dips and hollows of her smokin' hot body.

"Not hungry, bro?" Jake asked.

Ben blinked, and nodded. "Yeah." He took a big, juicy burger for himself and began to eat.

Tammy cut her burger in half before taking a bite. He watched her swallow, hearing a moan of pleasure from her.

"Wow, that's good," she said.

"I know." Harmony wiped her mouth. "Max and Ariel would give me a hard time for eating this much red meat."

"Max and Ariel?" Ben asked.

"My parents," Harmony said. "They're kind of hippy throwbacks."

"Yeah, I think they were born twenty years too late," Rick said.

"They run the rec café out on the nature trails, Ben," Tammy said. "Healthy snacks, rainforest coffee."

"Very West Coast," Cassie put in. "You would like it, I think."

Tammy's brows rose in question.

"Ben grew up in California," Harmony said in answer to her unasked question.

Tammy nodded, shooting him a smirk that did amazing things to her lips. He realized then that they really didn't know much about each other. He knew she was from South Jersey and had family up there. She knew he didn't have any family but these people sitting right here. And Bill, of course. That was it, though.

Before too long, lunch was eaten and Harmony brought out a container holding what Ben now thought of as Claire's perfect cookies. Tammy hadn't been joking when she'd said how precise a baker she was. And how good her treats were.

Talk continued around him, jokes and stories that were new to him. He smiled and nodded but pretty much kept quiet. What did he have to contribute to the conversation?

After taking one of Claire's pretty perfect oatmeal cookies, Tammy rose. "Well, I'm gonna take off."

Ben's head shot up. He caught her gaze and she gave him a small smile.

"Oh, okay," Harmony said, coming to her feet. "I'm so happy you came."

Tammy nodded. "Thanks again for inviting me."

Claire jumped up and wrapped Tammy in a hug, which Tammy returned with obvious ease. Those two were definitely tight. More complications.

"See you, Tammy," Cassie said.

Ben found himself on his feet, too. "Let me walk you out."

All of the Chapmans, except for little Nick, turned matching looks of interest in his direction. Ben ducked his head and followed Tammy back into the house.

"You know, I don't need an escort," she said, her voice low.

"I know." He couldn't resist putting his hand on the small of her back as they stepped out onto the front porch. He bent his head close to her ear, breathing in her spicy floral scent. "Remember, my mother raised me to be a gentleman, Tamara."

She arched a brow as she glanced over her shoulder. Their faces were very close now, and he watched as she licked her lips.

59

"Oh, yeah? That's a shame."

He stilled again, and then saw the glint in her eye. He laughed softly. "You got me."

Those full lips of hers curved in a wide smile. She then came to a stop on the bottom step, staring up at him for a second. "I guess I'll see you tomorrow?"

"Tomorrow?" He forced his gaze away from her mouth and thought for a second. "Yeah. At the Sales Center."

"You're meeting with Mr. Forbes?"

He nodded, but didn't say anything more. He still wasn't sure what the hell he was going to say to the guy. She waited for him to say something else, apparently, and then turned and walked to a little silver convertible parked behind Claire's prized Thunderbird.

"See you then," she said.

He stood there like an idiot, watching as she drove away toward whatever village she lived in here at Cypress. He knew she lived on property. Rick had told him that much.

He thought again about his upcoming meeting with Mr. Forbes. The guy wanted him on the job. Ben knew he should be grateful for the opportunity. It was a lot of change in a short amount of time, though. Losing his mother. Reconnecting with his father. Meeting his siblings. Did he really want to deal with a new job, too?

Grunting in frustration, he settled on one of the Adirondack chairs and stared at the lakeshore across the street. The park and dock were pretty quiet now. Couples strolled and a few families were out for walks, though. The air was still warm but he caught a bit of a cool breeze.

"Hey, bro."

He looked over to see Jake standing near the front door. "Hey, Jake."

Jake held up two opened bottles of beer. "When you didn't come back, I figured one of two things happened. Turns out I was right."

"Yeah?" Ben raised his brows and took one of the bottles. "What was the first thing?"

Jake grinned and settled in the chair beside his. "Tammy took you home, which would have surprised me."

"Why?" He took a long sip of his beer. "Or do I even want to know?"

"Tammy may be hot as hell," Jake said. "But she's not easy."

Ben thought again about the vision she'd made on the

lounge chair. And the way she'd teased him, too. She was quick. But easy? No friggin' way.

"So what's the other thing?"

Jake drank from his bottle, and then leaned back like Ben. "You have a lot to think about before your meeting with Forbes."

"You know about that?"

"Rick told me. What are you going to do?"

Ben blew out a breath. "I don't know. I know I should probably jump at the chance."

"If only to stay away from Boston, right?"

He caught Jake's knowing smile and couldn't help returning it. "You got that right."

"I say you listen to what Forbes offers. But I'm warning you. He's very persuasive."

"Are you saying he's the reason you stayed in Cypress?"

Jake got a light in his eyes now as he shook his head. "No, man. The reason is Claire, and I'm not a big enough fool to ever forget that."

Ben chuckled and saluted him with his beer. He grew quiet again, and his brother seemed to catch his mood. Several minutes passed as the two of them drank their beer in silence. It was nice. Comfortable.

He wouldn't think any more about Forbes and their meeting tomorrow. He wouldn't think about all the ways Tammy could complicate things for him here, either. No. He'd just sit here with his brother and think about nothing more than sharing a beer as the evening came.

That, and a hot, definitely not so easy Italian girl from Jersey.

Chapter 5

Tammy walked out of the coffee shop, holding a cup of pumpkin spice latte in each hand. She smiled her thanks to the guy who held open the door for her, earning a once-over she could have done without, and breathed in the delectable smell of cinnamon and nutmeg in the to-go cups. The coffee was Claire's favorite, and Tammy knew her friend could use a little cheering up. She'd still looked a little wistful as she watched Jake play with his nephew yesterday.

Tammy admitted, at least to herself, that the drink put her in the autumn spirit, too. While she didn't miss the heavy, wet snow Jersey got most winters she did miss the changing of the leaves every fall. Bringing the cup in her right hand closer, her latte, she gave it another sniff.

"Pleasure in a cup, am I right?" Lettie drawled from the courtyard of the shop.

Tammy smiled at Charlotte Fairfax, or Lettie as everyone in Cypress knew her. The lady was sitting court at her usual spot under her favorite crepe myrtle. Instead of her usual sweet tea, it seemed Lettie was enjoying the latest "drink of the season" from the coffee shop too. There was a stack of catalogues spread out on the table in front of her but Tammy knew Lettie wasn't shopping for clothes or shoes. Plants were the lady's thing, and the fall was the time to order bulbs, or so Lettie had told her.

"Hey there, Lettie." She crossed over to her. "You really saved me yesterday. Harmony loved the plant. Thank you again."

Lettie waved a hand. "Happy to help, dear."

Her blue eyes peered closely at her from under the silver bangs brushing over her brow. Tammy braced herself. You never knew what was going to come out of Lettie's mouth.

Lettie was a staple in the town center. That was for sure. As usual, the woman wore a large straw hat, a flower-print smock, denim overalls, and a pair of bright green Crocs. Tammy knew she was in her seventies but she looked closer to fifty. She claimed this was due to healthy living, big hats and the liberal application of sunscreen. She was outrageous and sweet, and knew every bit of gossip that could be found in Cypress. She was one of the reasons Tammy kept her business to herself. Dated outside of Cypress. Kept out of the Cypress fishbowl.

"Did you have a nice time at the Chapmans', dear?" Lettie asked.

Tammy nodded. "Very nice, thanks."

"Hmm. I wondered what kept you from the seashore when you stopped by yesterday, but I saw the reason for myself just this morning."

Tammy's stomach tightened. "Oh?"

Lettie dropped her chin a bit and raised her brows, her gaze a challenge. "I saw the newest Chapman to land in Cypress this morning, Tammy. Mighty fine looking young man, I must say."

Tammy gave Lettie a small smile and a nod, which was just the ammunition the woman needed.

"Maybe you'll finally get your own Chapman?" she asked.

Tammy gaped at her, and then looked around. The courtyard wasn't crowded even though the coffee shop itself was hopping, but she didn't want anyone to overhear that comment.

"I never wanted the other ones, Lettie."

Lettie nodded. "Oh, I know that. A smart girl knows when a man's eye settles elsewhere. But they sure are delightful to look at, am I right?"

"There's no denying that," Tammy said.

"And now another is in our midst. I hear he builds things." Lettie laughed softly. "Works with his hands."

Tammy flushed as she pictured Ben's big, capable-looking hands. "He's an architect."

"Oh, I know." Lettie winked, and Tammy was reminded again that very little escaped the woman's notice. "With that fine physique, though? I'm sure he gets into the thick of it."

Tammy coughed to cover up her laughter. Lettie didn't need any encouragement. "Maybe," she allowed. "Well, I'm off to work. Picking out bulbs, I take it?"

Lettie clicked her tongue, and then smiled. "A diversion, Tammy? Oh, all right. You hurry off to work."

Tammy lifted one of the coffee cups in salute, and then turned to face the street. As she crossed toward the Sales Center, she saw a shiny red Jeep pulling into the crushed-shell parking lot to the left of it. She saw the dark-haired guy step out of it, and guessed Ben must have rented the Wrangler. It suited him. It was rugged and hot.

Keeping her eyes on the fine picture he made today in his khakis and crisp gray oxford shirt, she reasoned he looked more Boston than California this morning. The neat, dark blue tie didn't hurt, either.

"Hey there, Ben," she called.

He glanced over and a big smile spread across his features. That one dimple peeped into view and she felt her stomach flutter. "Hey there, Tammy."

He stepped in front of her as they mounted the steps and held open the door for her.

"Thanks," she said.

She stepped through and he came up beside her. Leaning closer, he breathed in. "Pumpkin?"

She shrugged. "Seemed about right this morning."

Ben tilted his head to the side. "I'll have to try it."

She lifted the cup in her right hand. "Try mine."

His eyes sparkled and he took her up on her offer. She'd only been teasing, but he took the cup and drank. Closing his eyes, he let out a little moan. "That's good." He looked at her again. "Hot and spicy."

A flush spread over her in a wave. "Yeah."

He handed her the cup again. "Who's the other one for?"

"Claire. It's her one weakness."

He smiled. They stood there staring again, like they had last night on Harmony's front porch. He was the first to come to his senses, apparently.

"Well, let me go find Mr. Forbes," he said.

She nodded like an idiot and watched him head down the corridor. Closing her eyes now, she took a breath and lifted her cup to her lips. Yeah, it tasted like pumpkin spice but she could detect a hint of Ben on the lid. Freshness teased her tongue as she stroked the spot where his lips had just been.

"Are you going to kiss that all morning?" Claire asked with a smile as she stepped out of her office.

Tammy chuckled. "Nope." She held out the untouched cup. "This one is yours."

Claire's eyes rounded and her smile widened. "You're a Monday morning angel!"

Tammy laughed softly. "I'll take that."

Claire motioned her to follow as she went into her office.

"What's up?" Tammy asked her.

"I just wanted to thank you for coming yesterday."

"Why all the gratitude?" She shut Claire's door and leaned on the corner of her desk. "I feel like I really didn't add much to the party."

Claire blinked at her. "Are you serious? You seemed to bring Ben out of himself, at least a little bit. Jake said you'd be good for him."

Tammy shook her head as her heart started to pound. "Oh, no. I'm not a candidate for matchmaking, Claire. Besides, Ben and I barely know each other and he has a lot to deal with right now."

Claire leveled a look at her. "And how do you know that little tidbit, hmm? You've been talking to him."

Tammy started to argue, and then held up her free hand. "All right. We've been talking. He's staying at the inn and I was using their beach yesterday morning."

Claire waved a finger at her. "Naughty."

"Yeah, well I was just using the beach. Nothing naughty, believe me."

"For now."

"Will you please stop? I heard enough about it from Lettie just now."

"Lettie? And just what does our resident spark-spotter have to say about you and Ben?"

"Nothing that bears repeating. Wishful thinking on her part, I'm sure."

"Yeah, and I didn't catch you watching Ben all yesterday afternoon."

Tammy straightened. "I'm out of the little girls' room. If you're finished scheming?"

Claire shrugged. "All right, I'll stop. For now. You're taking him on a tour later?"

"Yes."

Claire took a sip of her latte, her brows arched. "Just asking."

Tammy opened her door. "I'll catch you later. Lunch at the tavern?"

"I brought lunch."

"You always do."

Claire just smiled. Her frugality was one of her defining features and Tammy knew where she was coming from. If Tammy had Claire's father to look after, she'd watch every penny too.

Stepping out into the hall, she headed down to her office. She eyed Mr. Forbes' closed door and wondered how Ben was faring. Her boss never delivered anything less than a full-court press. Would Ben take him up on his offer? And what if he did agree to work at Cypress? Where would that leave her?

In deep trouble, that's where. She liked Ben. Liked talking to him and liked being with him. She'd never been so attracted to a guy before. It didn't matter. She'd just put on her big-girl panties and keep her hands off this newest Chapman. He might say he wasn't into family but she caught glimpses of just that connection yesterday at Harmony and Rick's house. He wanted it. Maybe even needed it. Either way, that put him out of reach.

He was forever and she so was not.

For a second, she wished she was but that wouldn't last very long. She just wasn't wired for commitment.

***

"Ben, I couldn't be happier with your decision."

Mr. Forbes held out his hand and Ben shook it. He wasn't quite sure what had just happened, but he found himself returning the man's smile. Jake hadn't been kidding. The guy made it very hard to say no. Ben would have input and a voice, and be in charge of each step of the new green development. And the pay wasn't bad, either.

"I'm looking forward to working on the new project, Mr. Forbes."

"Great." Forbes stood and crossed to the door of his office. "Let me go find Tammy for you and you can start that tour."

"I can find her." He'd probably smell her first. Flowers and spice, like her coffee this morning. "Is there anywhere in particular you want her to take me?"

Forbes furrowed his brow for a second. "I think she should give you the customary tour and then head on over to the green neighborhood site."

"Sounds good." Ben opened the door. "I think I'll enjoy

72

working here at Cypress."

The other man grinned now. "And you'll be close to your family."

"Yes." Ben didn't quite know how he felt about that, but he was committed now. Besides, his siblings had been nothing but welcoming. "When do you want me to start on the project?"

"Come in on Wednesday morning and we'll have an office ready for you. You're going to have to go to the Cypress Institute and meet with the director, too. They're going to have a lot of input on this project."

Ben had heard about the Cypress Institute. Those were the "tree-huggers" his father had talked about back in Boston. It was clear Bill was clueless, but he insisted that the Institute impacted the bottom line. Ben hadn't been there yet but both Harmony and his future brother-in-law Ty worked there.

"Sounds good. Thank you again, Mr. Forbes."

He left Mr. Forbes and started down the hall to where he knew Tammy's office to be. Voices reached him as he passed the breakroom and he peered inside. It was set up typically, with a couple of round tables with a handful of chairs at each. Jake's wife, Claire, and that blond guy who worked with Tammy sat inside. Ben started to pull back but his sister-in-law caught him.

"Ben!" She waved him inside and, by the way she smiled, there was no refusing her. "Come in, come in."

"Hey, Claire."

"Do you know Ollie?" Claire asked.

Ben nodded and lifted his chin at the blond guy. "We've met. Hey."

"Hey, Ben." Ollie's blue eyes sparkled. "So, is it true?"

"Is what true?" Claire asked.

"Ben here's going to join the team."

Claire clasped her hands, her face alight. "Really? Jake will be happy you're going to be sticking around."

Ben flushed a little. "I'm working on the green development."

"That's great, Ben," Claire said. "Right up your alley."

"And our girl is giving him the ten cent tour today," Ollie put in.

Claire's eyes narrowed a little as her mouth kicked up on one side. "Yeah. I'd heard."

Ben wondered at that. She'd heard from Tammy? Or from Mr. Forbes?

"Where's Tammy now?" Ben asked.

"Out on tour," Ollie said. "An innocent family of four, soon

74

to fall victim to the charms of Cypress Corners."

"And the charms of Tammy," Ben said without thinking.

They both stared at him and Ben managed to keep his expression even. There was no arguing that the girl had skills of persuasion. God knew he was ready to buy whatever she was selling.

Just to have something to do, he crossed to the fridge and grabbed himself a bottle of water. "Do you know when she'll be back?" he asked, cracking open his bottle.

"Should be just a little while. She's been gone for about a half an hour already."

"So the tours are short, then," Ben said.

"Depends," Ollie said.

"On what?" Ben had to know.

"On just how much they want to see."

He met Ollie's gaze and easily saw the laughter there. A smile teased Ben's lips. Making sure he appeared like the laid-back Cali guy they probably expected, Ben settled into a chair at their table. He took a long sip of his water. "All right, then."

"I have numbers to crunch." Claire popped out of her seat and touched Ben on the shoulder. "Enjoy your tour, Ben."

"Thanks." He caught Ollie's gaze again. "I'm sure I will."

75

Ollie waited until Claire was gone, and then let out a whistle. "You're bad, Ben Chapman."

"That's what they tell me."

Ollie's brows arched comically. "You have something, you know that? Of course you know that. You're a Chapman, for God's sake."

Ben chuckled. "What does that mean?"

"You guys are all sex-on-a-stick, my man." He sighed and rolled his eyes. "Too bad none of you play on my team."

Ben laughed out loud. "You're a little bad yourself."

"Oh, you don't know the half of it." Ollie glanced at his watch and pushed his chair back. "I have a tour in about five minutes. Catch you later, Ben Chapman."

Ben nodded and drank more of his water. So this was where he was going to work. For the next few months at least. The other people who worked here seemed pretty nice, and he would get to hang with his brothers a little bit too. There was also the very big draw of seeing Tammy every day.

What Cypress Corners had planned was very intriguing. He'd gotten his share of the development's story. The connection and commitment to nature that was unusual for an undertaking of its size. It was a beautiful place, though. He just had to think about the lake view from his room at the Cypress Inn to realize that the tamed yet natural landscape was well-suited to the developers' and the Cypress Institute's vision.

"Hey, there," Tammy said.

Her voice stroked over him and he smiled even before he lifted his head. She stood in the doorway of the breakroom, crisp and pressed and as hot as he'd ever seen her. Talk about a vision.

"Hey, Tammy." He stood, catching the way her hazel eyes roamed over the front of him. "Are you ready for me?"

Chapter 6

Tammy's mouth dropped open for a second, but she closed it with a snap. Ollie had warned her just a few minutes ago that this guy had hidden depths. She hadn't needed Ollie to tell her that, though. She knew precisely the danger Ben posed to everything she'd built for herself.

Putting on her just-this-side-of-sexy salesperson polish, she gave him her professional smile. "Yep. The cart is charged up and we're ready to roll."

"Mr. Forbes wants you to take me out to where the green project will be built."

Tammy nodded, turning away from those gorgeous blue-gray eyes to grab herself a bottle of water from the fridge. "He filled me in."

"Cool."

Facing him again, she watched as he removed his tie. He leaned his head back, unbuttoning the top two buttons of his oxford shirt. He had a nice, strong neck. She suspected she could hold on tight to him while he drove her crazy with those big hands of his. She knew that as sure as she knew she could drive him just as crazy.

Shake it off, girl. She straightened her shoulders. "Okay, then. Let's go."

Ben waved her in front of him as he tucked his tie into his front pocket. She caught his scent, then. That freshness she'd tasted on her coffee cup lid. Delicious.

He held the door of the Sales Center open for her as he had earlier, and she walked out into the September morning. There was a touch of crispness to the air but it was still very warm. They would both need the bottles of water they'd brought this morning.

The four-passenger golf cart was outfitted for touring guests, prospective residents and investors. Comfy leather seats, a jaunty green, white and burgundy striped awning, and big fat tires that made the ride smooth. Ben eased his big body into the seat next to the driver's, and Tammy wasn't surprised. Of course he would sit right next to her.

She started the quiet electric motor, and then buckled her seatbelt. "Buckle up, Big Ben."

He chuckled as he did so. "Big Ben, huh?"

She grinned. "Ollie pinned that one on you."

"Hmm." His eyes sparkled at her.

"Do I even want to know what you're thinking?" she asked

79

him.

"I was just thinking that maybe you'd want to find out if he's right."

Her face flushed hot and she shook her head at him. "Stop that. I have a job to do here."

He leaned back and waved a hand. "Drive on, Miss Donato."

She turned the street-legal vehicle onto the road, waving at Lettie as she drove past the coffee shop. Lettie raised a hand, and her brows, but Tammy simply smirked and headed toward the neighborhoods to the west side of the sprawling property.

"You're familiar with Rick and Harmony's neighborhood, I imagine," she said.

"Yep. Really nice. Right across from the main lakeshore with that big lot. Great spot."

"There are a couple other villages set up like theirs. North of the town square behind the front nine of the golf course. Most of the neighborhoods are more modest in size and more densely built, though. Have you been to Claire and Jake's place?"

"Once. The last time I was here. But I don't remember much about the neighborhood."

She pulled the wheel to the left after a short stop. "Then

let's head that way." She winked at him. "Westward, ho."

He smiled. "This is going to be an adventure, isn't it?"

She glanced at him before facing the road once more. "Brace yourself, Ben. This is the easy stuff."

"Easy," he murmured.

His voice had gone all soft and she ignored the way it made her feel. All tingly and hot. Luckily, they soon drove through the more populated village where Claire and Jake made their home.

"There's your brother's place," she said, indicating the modest yet pretty one-story house nestled in one of the more densely-populated villages of Cypress Corners.

It was a two-bedroom bungalow with deep moldings and hardwood floors and Claire had it furnished with the bare minimum. Still, it was comfy and homey and very well-suited to her best friend and her husband.

"The houses in this neighborhood have all the classic trimmings and high-end finishes as the ones in Rick and Harmony's, but they're built on a smaller scale."

"And on a smaller lot," Ben said.

Tammy nodded. "Even though the homes look classic and timeless, they're outfitted with forward-thinking tech and amenities."

"Yes. I really like that. The classic look is very welcome and familiar but the homeowners don't have to sacrifice convenience."

She shot him a look, a smile teasing her mouth. "Exactly. You know, your project will take that concept even further."

"I know." He grew quiet for a second. "I hope I'm up to the challenge."

Keeping her eyes forward, she decided to finally satisfy her curiosity. She knew if you didn't look someone dead-on they just might open up a little bit. It was how she learned just what prospective residents were looking for and what they really didn't want in their new home or community. Today, though? She couldn't resist using the trick to learn more about this compelling guy.

"You come with impeccable references, Ben. Mr. Forbes couldn't say enough good things about you even before you decided to meet with him."

"Yeah." His voice sounded a little flat.

"So what's the deal? You don't want to work down here in Florida? I admit, it's not California."

"No, that's not it. It's really nice down here. What I've seen of it anyway."

"And there's your family."

"Yeah," he said again.

She risked a look at him out of the corner of her eye. His brow was furrowed and there were lines bracketing that full mouth of his.

"Ben, your family is nothing like mine."

He angled his body to face her, his arm draped over the back of her seat. "Tell me about the New Jersey Donatos, then."

She laughed and shook her head. "No way. All I'm saying is, your family is warm and welcoming. They make you a part of things."

"And yours doesn't?"

That question brought her up short. "Actually, they do. When I go up north, that is. But they're also intrusive and overpowering." She gave a shiver. "A little smothering."

She caught his smile and returned the expression.

"They don't sound so bad," he said.

"They're not." She blew a breath, reaching up to tuck a strand of hair behind her ear. "They're very loving and kind. Good people."

"And you never go back home to see them."

"I do." She blinked back the tears that suddenly pricked at

the back of her eyes. "Usually around the holidays."

"Christmas?"

"Yeah, Christmas. We do it all. Feast of the Seven Fishes, Midnight Mass. All the trimmings."

"Feast of the what?"

"Seven Fishes." She drove on out of Claire and Jake's neighborhood and turned to the lakeshore. "Traditionally, you couldn't eat meat Christmas Eve. So Italians, still determined to eat their weight in food, cook seven different kinds of seafood that night."

"That sounds pretty good to me. I grew up eating at least seven different kinds of seafood."

She threw a smile at him. "Not like this, you didn't. Let's just say there's lots of cheese, olive oil and tomato sauce."

"Still sounds good. Do you cook?"

"Um, actually I do."

She was surprised she admitted this to him. Not many people knew she liked to cook. Even Claire didn't know how many nights Tammy spent adjusting her family's recipes for just herself.

"Italian?" he asked.

She smirked at him this time. "I'm Italian. Anything I cook

is Italian."

A deep chuckle came from him. "Smartass."

She laughed. "Yes, I can make the usual. Lasagna. Bolognese. Puttanesca. Beef braciole."

"That's the usual?" He spread his legs a bit, brushing her thigh with his. "Maybe I'll have to stay at your place and you can feed me."

Inexplicably, she imagined him sitting in her kitchen as she fed him one delicious dish after another. She'd never cooked for a guy. Never. She wouldn't start now.

"My mother raised me to be a lady," she said, turning his frequent "gentleman" comments back on him.

"Yeah, we'll see."

There was a promise in his eyes and she sucked in a breath. Ooh, that look made her want to cook for him and then have her way with him. She couldn't risk that. It would be fantastic, of course. She knew what she was doing and she could tell he was no slouch in that department. But it would also be very comfortable. Domestic.

And that scared the living daylights out of her.

***

Ben stared at Tammy's profile as her expression shifted. It

was subtle, but he caught it. She'd been warm and teasing and now she was shuttered. Professional. Was it his cooking comment? Or his decidedly un-subtle hint that he would stay over at her place and soon.

"Show me your place," he said.

She gave him a quick look, her eyes wide. "What?"

"Your neighborhood, Tammy."

She laughed a little, and then nodded. "Okay. I have a townhouse not far from the town center."

He leaned back again, putting a touch of ease in his posture that he hoped she would pick up on. He didn't want to make her nervous. He wasn't that guy. He wasn't pushy, and he'd never had to be. But letting Tammy set the pace? What if she kept him in the friend zone indefinitely, which he felt looming large in front of them? No friggin' way.

"Show me," he said again.

She turned the wheel and the golf cart bounced a little as she drove over a curb. He hid his smile. She wasn't as cool as she was pretending to be right now.

"My townhouse is nestled near the outside of the neighborhood. With views of the golf course."

"Nice."

He sat up as the rows of townhouses came into view. They looked like separate residences, which appealed to him. Classic details were evident in this village as well. Columns and railings framed the porches and deep eaves gave the homes a rich look. They appeared to be large, too.

"How many square feet?" he asked.

"They range from eighteen hundred to just over two thousand."

"Yours is two thousand, I'm guessing?"

She threw him an easy smile. "You know it. And an end unit, too."

"Got yourself a deal, did you?"

She winked, and he thought she looked adorable as well as hot.

"Hey, I'm tight with the developer."

Ben barked out a laugh. "Forbes knows how to keep his people happy."

They pulled to a stop in front of a large, end unit. It was a soft green with cream trim, with a glossy deep-red front door. There was a wood-and-wrought-iron bench set to one side of the door piled with colorful pillows.

"Really nice. Give me a tour?"

She nibbled on her lower lip, looking unsure for the first time since he'd met her. "If you want one."

He was tempted to press her. To get her to admit she wanted him in her house as much as he wanted to be there. She looked nervous, though. It was weird, but he didn't want to push it.

"Another time," he said. "Maybe for one of your Italian masterpiece meals."

Her smile was quick and wide. "Maybe."

Maybe? From the promise in her voice, it sounded more like *definitely.*

She pulled away from the curb. "How about we head over to your project site?"

"Sounds good."

The landscape shifted subtly as they left the more populated part of Cypress. The wind caught in her hair, blowing it around her face and a little bit in his. It was silky soft, and he caught her scent.

"Your site is to the west of Rick and Harmony's neighborhood, Ben. Past the inn."

"That will be convenient."

"So you plan on staying at the inn?"

"It suits me for now."

"You know, I can arrange a house for you if you like. I did that for Rick when he first came down here."

A house meant more roots, and he just wasn't ready for that yet. "No, I'm good."

She nodded, tucking a strand of hair behind one perfect ear again. "Okay. This neighborhood will have several lots facing the lakeshore, as I'm sure Mr. Forbes showed you."

"We didn't get into too many details, but he did show me on the scale model where the project would be set."

The cart bounced over the rough path as it made its way to Ben's new project. He felt a tingle of anticipation as he began to envision the setting with homes and green space. He straightened, the familiar thrill of potential coursing through him like lightning.

She stopped the cart and turned to face him. "What do you think?"

His mouth dropped open but he couldn't form an answer to her very simple question. For the first time since his mother died he felt that spark that had always driven him in his work. That he'd always taken for granted. His heart began to pound and he felt as if electricity coursed through his body in a rush.

He turned to Tammy, a big grin on his face.

She tilted her head to one side, a smile curving her lips. "I take it you like it?"

He was without words for a long minute, and then he grabbed her to him. "God, you have no idea."

She felt so good against him, tucking her face right between his neck and shoulder. She was soft and warm, and he wanted to hold her forever. Longed to tell her just what this moment meant to him. This project could put him back on the path he hadn't seen for nearly a year. Damn, it was staggering.

"Ben?"

There was a question in her voice. A softness that spoke of both confusion and need. Pulling back, he ran his gaze over her face. She was flushed and gorgeous and he couldn't have stopped himself if he tried. He kissed her.

Her lips were sweet and hot, like her. Moaning a little, he slanted his mouth over hers and teased her lips with his tongue. She opened for him, making a soft whimper as she stroked his tongue with hers. Her breasts, even in her polished professional shirt, rubbed against his chest in a way that really got him going. Damn, he was so turned on from just a kiss he could hardly breathe.

Pulling back, he cupped her face with his hands. "Tamara."

Chapter 7

She licked her lips and he made that hot little moan again. "I love when you say my name like that," she whispered.

Bringing his face to the side of her neck, he said it again. His jaw was a little scratchy but that only added to the heat between them. She had to stop this. She was a professional. She was giving him a tour, for God's sake! But before she could make even a token attempt to pull away, he pressed his face between her breasts.

"You smell so damn good," he rasped.

She peeked around quickly and saw there was no one around to see whatever it was he planned to do to her. She wanted to give in. Wanted him to taste her. To tease her. It was crazy, but this man was like none she'd known before.

His fingers were quick. A few buttons undone and he bared her pretty purple lace bra. She gripped his shoulders as he pulled one cup aside to free one breast. He took her aching nipple in his mouth and suckled.

"Oh, God." She arched, her fingers running through his hair as she kept him right where she wanted him to be. "That feels so good."

He licked and nibbled as his hand trailed up under her skirt to tease the lace covering her. She felt damp. Swollen. His fingers shook a little as he eased inside of her, and she knew he was as amped up as she was.

It only took a few strokes and she was bucking against him. Her climax tore through her and she bit back on a scream. It was way too quick and stunned her breathless.

"Tamara," he whispered, leaving her breast at last to press his brow to hers. "Damn, you're sweet."

She opened her eyes, her breath coming fast, and stared at him. His eyes were dark and his lips parted. She bit down on her lip again. "That's a first for me."

He kissed her again. "I'm sorry, but I had to touch you."

She blinked at him as he licked those clever fingers of his. Oh, that was hot. He was hot. And she was half-naked and nearly on his lap.

Jumping back into her seat, she adjusted her clothes as she frantically looked around. Her pulse raced as she thought of just what might happen to her career if anyone saw what she'd just done with Ben.

"There's no one around, Tammy," he said.

She buttoned her blouse and closed her eyes, taking in a

cleansing breath. "What was that?" she asked, chancing a look at him again.

"I couldn't help myself." He didn't look like he regretted it in the least, though. Not telling from the grin spread across his handsome face. "I was just so… I can't explain."

"I saw it, Ben. That excitement in your eyes before you even touched me."

"I could see it all, Tammy." He rubbed his hands over his face, that smile firmly in place. "Clear as day. The houses. The paths. The green spaces. The whole damn neighborhood. It's going to be beautiful."

She tried to process what he was saying. This was what he did, wasn't it? How was this project so different from his work in California?

He was stroking her arm again, just shy of pulling her onto his lap. She couldn't do that. Couldn't give in again. No way.

"I've never done this before, Ben. I wasn't kidding when I said that."

His expression sobered a bit. "I didn't think you were. You're not easy. Jake wasn't wrong when he told me that."

She faced him again. "Jake said that about me?"

Ben shrugged. "He knew I was attracted to you. Hell, I'd

have to be dead not to be. I think he wanted to make sure I didn't hurt you."

She thought for a second. "He's a good guy. I'm glad he's with Claire."

"They both seem to care about you."

A warmth spread through her, gentler than the fire Ben had set inside of her, but still really nice. "Yeah. I guess they do."

She glanced at the front of his pants and saw his pretty impressive hard-on through the fabric. "Seems you've got a problem there, Big Ben."

He chuckled and settled back in his seat, bracing his legs apart. "I'll survive."

"Oh, yeah?"

"I'll just think about specs and plans and all the ways I'm going to change this plot of land into a neighborhood that's environmentally responsible and a great place to live."

She heard that excitement in his voice again. He was pumped for the project and that was very hot, too.

"That sounds like you're all in," she said. "Are you?"

He studied her for a second and she realized in just what direction her question might be taken. "I'm all in."

And just what did he mean by that? Unable to resist, she

leaned in for another delicious kiss, and then started the cart again.

"Let's get you back to the Sales Center." She tilted her chin in the direction of his groin. "Do you think you'll be presentable by the time we get there or should I drive around a little bit longer?" she teased.

He chuckled. "Believe me, Tammy. If I drive around a little bit longer with you I'll need more than a redirection of my thoughts to get back in control."

She dipped her head, her cheeks heating. He was so good for her ego, even if he was bad for her in every other respect. Bad for her sanity and maybe even her career, given the fact that she'd just nearly screamed her orgasm out in the open in a company golf cart.

By the time they rolled toward the town center, her body was back in control. Her head was a whole different matter. It was on all tangled up in everything he'd said. His commitment to the job was clear. As for the rest of it? She had no idea.

"Here we are," she said, pulling to a stop in front of the Sales Center.

He rubbed his hands on his thighs, taking in a breath. "I want to see where this goes, Tammy."

95

"Where what goes? The project?"

He arched one brow.

A flutter of nerves struck her and she gripped the steering wheel. "We're friends, Ben."

He shook his head. "I'd say we left the friend zone somewhere back there. What's next?"

"Oh, Ben. I'm not ready for whatever might be next."

"What do you mean?"

She couldn't tell him he had "forever" written all over him. He'd think she was nuts to expect that after a little foreplay in a golf cart. What was worse, she'd have to tell him that she couldn't want anything less than she wanted forever.

Whenever she told a guy that they either thought she was strange, or worse, that she was lying in an effort to "snag" him. It was a catch-22 and she couldn't deal with whatever version Ben might throw her way.

"I value my job," she said instead. "I'm very good at it, and I can't afford to lose it."

"I wouldn't cause you any trouble, Tammy. Not on a bet."

He looked so sincere. His gaze was even and his smile long gone. Could she give him a chance just to see what would happen?

She climbed out of the cart and ran her hands over her hair. Taking a quick glance down the front of her she saw she still appeared pressed and put together, except for some slight wrinkles on the front of her skirt. No one would be able to guess what caused them, though. Ben's hands hiking her skirt up to her waist. His magical fingers on her flesh. The memory nearly made her moan.

He stepped out, stretching to his full impressive height. He braced his hands on the awning, leaning slightly closer to her. With his head tilted to one side, those blue-gray eyes of his so intense, he was hard to ignore. He was so tempting. She never denied herself anything, did she? She found she just couldn't start now.

"I'm driving next time," she said.

He blinked at her. "But you drove this time."

It was her turn to arch a brow at him.

A slow smile spread across his face. "Just name the time and place, Tamara."

Oh, the way he said her name. She knew her cheeks were pink but maybe that could be attributed to the ride in the warm September air.

Unable to keep a smile off her flushed face, she sailed back into the Sales Center and bumped right into Ollie.

"Whoa there, girl." He pulled back, crossing his arms over his chest. "And what put that smile on your face?"

She waved a hand. "Another great tour, Ollie. Nothing more."

He glanced over her shoulder and she resisted following his line of vision. She knew he saw Ben out there. That was obvious when he looked back at her with a smirk.

"Nothing more, huh?"

Instead of giving him another lame answer, she tweaked his nose and went into her office, shutting the door tight behind her. A little time was all she needed to process just what happened today. Ben was magic. She knew he would be. From the first second she'd seen him. He was dangerous, too. To everything she'd built for herself.

She was prepared for whatever happened. At least she hoped so.

"Name the time and place, huh?" She smiled to herself. "Sooner than you think, Big Ben."

***

Ben stared at the doors of the Sales Center long after Tammy disappeared inside. He shouldn't have been surprised back there in the golf cart. When the heat flared so fast and hot between them. She was hesitant to go for more, though. He sure as hell wasn't. He was still half-hard.

Turning away, he headed for the coffee shop. It would give him something to occupy himself as he worked his mind through everything that happened. Not what happened between him and Tammy. That was for later, when he was alone in the shower with nothing but memories to drive him home. No. He was stunned by the surge of creative energy that had rushed over him out at the new worksite. He'd never felt that kind of energy before. Even with his biggest, most lucrative jobs in Santa Cruz.

"Hello there, Ben Chapman."

He glanced over to see an older woman eyeing him from the courtyard. From her sweet southern drawl, he figured this must be the legendary Lettie. She was dressed like a lady gardener, with overalls and a big straw hat perched on her head. The long look she gave him almost made him feel naked.

"Hello," he said.

"Lettie Fairfax, Ben."

She held out a hand and he took it, bowing his head a little. "A pleasure to meet you, Lettie."

She withdrew her hand to fan herself as she leaned back a

bit. "I wasn't wrong, was I?"

"About?"

"About you, dear boy. Our newest Chapman is just as steamy hot as his brothers."

Ben felt his face heat but he smiled at the lady. "I suppose I should say thank you."

"Seems to me I should be thanking you."

He grinned and she brought a hand to her throat.

"Be still my heart, you have a dimple."

"Guilty."

"Hmm." Her gaze grew thoughtful. "Seems our Tammy is in trouble."

At the mention of Tammy's name, he could think of all kinds of trouble he would enjoy getting her into. "How so?"

"I saw her with you, Ben. Just a little bit ago, actually. You spell trouble with a capital T."

"I would never do anything to hurt Tammy."

She studied him with her sharp blue eyes, her lips pursed. "I believe you're sincere. But there's no telling what a mess you all can tumble into if you're not careful."

She wasn't wrong, but he didn't want to think about all the reasons he shouldn't get involved with Tammy. Not right now.

"I'm always careful, Lettie," he assured her.

She gave a slow shake of her head. "Now that, Ben Chapman, is a damn shame."

That brought a laugh out of him and he bowed slightly to her. "Good day, ma'am."

She waved a hand. "Go on with you. I can tell you have charm to spare but you shouldn't waste any of it on me."

Nodding, he turned from her and continued on to the coffee shop.

"Hey, bro," Jake said behind him.

Ben turned around to face his brother. Jake looked a little mussed and Ben figured he must have been working on his adventure trails personally. It was another thing they had in common. He liked getting dirty on the jobsite, too.

"Hey, Jake." He made his way back to the brick sidewalk. "What's up?"

Jake tilted his head at the Sales Center. "How'd the tour go?"

Flashes of images filled Ben's mind as he recalled how sweet it was holding Tammy in his arms as she came apart. He cleared his throat. "Good."

Jake nodded. "You know, you should take one of Ty's eco-tours."

That perked up Ben's ears. "Eco-tours?"

"Yeah, you know. Tamed wilderness stuff. He's the one for it, too. Guy's a damn wild-animal whisperer."

"Hmm. He works at the Institute, right?"

Jake nodded, shoving his hands in the front of his cargo shorts. "Yeah, but he doesn't spend much time there. He's a field guy."

"Sounds like a man after my own heart."

Jake grinned. "That was what I figured." He scratched his chin. "Hey, what are you doing tonight?"

"Tonight?" He thought for a second. Not doing Tammy, he was pretty sure. "I don't have anything planned," he told Jake.

"Me, Claire, Cassie and Ty are going to the tavern for dinner tonight, if you want to join."

"That sounds great. Thanks."

Jake gripped Ben's shoulder and then gave him a pat. "Sure thing."

The physical contact was jarring, but not the action itself. No. It was what he'd felt in response to Jake's easy gesture. It felt good. Right. He found himself returning the gesture and the smile on his brother's face told him Jake felt it too.

"See you around six." Jake headed in the direction of the Sales Center, his face still turned toward Ben. "I'm going to go bug my wife."

Ben chuckled. "See you later, Jake."

Jake raised a hand and crossed the street. Ben stared off at the Clubhouse for a minute. The tavern was adjacent to the fancy restaurant. It was comfortable and set up like a pub. Good, hearty food and a nice atmosphere. When he'd eaten there with his siblings on his first visit, he'd preferred it to the fancier restaurant they'd also visited. The Clubhouse was more their father's speed. Even though he could appreciate the architecture and trimmings, not to mention the killer views of the golf course from just about every angle, it was so not Ben's scene. Yet another difference he had from Bill. And a similarity to his siblings.

"You okay, Big Ben?" Ollie asked.

Ben blinked and started when he saw Ollie standing right in front of him. "Ah, hi Ollie."

"You looked a little lost there."

Ben shook his head. "Nope. Not lost at all."

"Tammy said you really liked the new project site."

Ben grinned. "It's amazing, really. I can't wait to get

started."

Ollie blinked at him. "I can tell. You look pretty jazzed."

"I guess I am." He clapped Ollie on the shoulder like he had with Jake. "Catch you later, Ollie. I have a lot of reading to do if I'm starting on Wednesday."

"You'll be working at the Sales Center starting on Wednesday?"

"Yeah. Why?"

Ollie just smiled. "No reason. Working the whole day, are you?"

"I'll have to. There's a lot to learn and lot to plan out."

And for the first time in what felt like forever, he couldn't wait to set up his workspace and get started.

Chapter 8

Tammy shut down her computer and leaned back in her chair. It had taken most of the afternoon, but she'd finally been able to put Ben and the amazing things she'd felt in his arms out of her mind. At least she'd been able to focus as she gave a few tours this afternoon. It helped that she kept far away from the new project site on those tours. She'd never be able to keep from blushing if she had to drive past the spot where she'd lost all her marbles.

"Ready to call it a day?" Claire asked, leaning into Tammy's office.

Tammy gave her a smile. "So ready. Monday really lived up to its name."

"It sure looked like it was hopping there for a while."

"Yeah. Maybe we can bring Cassie back on staff to run some tours."

Tammy was only kidding there. Cassie had been an abysmal tour guide. She'd even driven her cart right off the path once, scaring the crap out of her unsuspecting prospects.

Claire laughed. "I don't think anybody wants that. Besides, Jake loves having her out at the Adventure Trails with him."

"He sure seems too." Tammy stood and flicked her hair over her shoulder. "I guess I'll see you tomorrow to do it all over again."

Claire nodded and then snapped her fingers, her eyes round. "Oh, you know what?"

Tammy blew out a breath. Something had Claire all excited and Tammy couldn't begin to guess what it was. Did she even want to know? "What?" she asked Claire.

"Jake and I are eating at the tavern with Ty and Cassie. Do you want to join us?"

"Join the four of you? So I can watch you bill and coo all over each other? No thanks."

Claire stepped back as Tammy closed and locked her office. "Come on. What are you going to do if you go home?"

"Relax." Tammy walked toward the lobby. "Maybe have a glass of wine. Put my feet up. The usual."

"Sounds a little tame for you, doesn't it?"

Tammy shot her a look. "It's a Monday, Claire."

"True." Claire grabbed onto her arm, her hold gentle yet firm. Like her. "Come on, Tammy. Come to dinner with us."

"Why would you want me to be a fifth wheel?" The truth struck her then. Clear as crystal. "Oh, very sneaky. Ben's going to be there, isn't he?"

Her friend blushed as Tammy had fully expected, confirming her suspicions. "Tammy, just—"

Tammy held up a hand. "Look. I like Ben." She really liked Ben, but she wasn't going to admit that to his sister-in-law. "But I don't want a setup and I really doubt he wants one."

"It's not a setup."

Tammy's lip curled. "Please."

"All right it's a setup, but only for dinner." Claire placed her hand over her heart. "You have my word."

Tammy crossed her arms. "Your word, huh?"

Claire gave her a solemn nod. "Come to the tavern?"

"All right." When Claire lit up from head to toe, Tammy shook her finger at her. "Don't get any ideas, Claire. I'm warning you."

Claire beamed a smile at her for a split second before sobering her expression. "No ideas, Tammy."

Tammy followed Claire's lead out of the Sales Center, turning to the Clubhouse and the adjacent tavern. What would Ben think when she showed up? Never mind that. How would she face him after what they'd done on their tour? After what she'd said to him before bidding him goodbye? Next time she'd drive, she'd told him. Well, this was certainly next time.

A thrill of anticipation went through her. She could admit to herself that she was looking forward to seeing him again. Those incredible eyes of his. That smile that teased his well-formed lips and brought out that dimple.

Jake, Cassie and Ty were seated at the bar when Tammy and Claire joined them.

"Hey, Tammy," Cassie said with a smile. "I didn't know you were joining us."

Tammy shot a knowing look in Claire's direction, and then shrugged. "I was coerced."

Ty laughed, raising his beer bottle in salute. "Yeah, the Chapmans do that." He winked at his bride-to-be. "Not that I'm not happy with how things turned out."

Cassie nudged him with her elbow, and then kissed his cheek. "Sweet-talker."

Tammy laughed and sat on the stool beside Cassie. "How are the wedding plans going?"

Cassie rolled her eyes. "Set, thank God. Ceremony out at the far lakeshore and reception to follow at the Clubhouse."

"I'd have it here in the tavern, if my mother wouldn't kill me," Ty said.

"How is your mother?" Claire asked.

Ty's mother had fibromyalgia and, from what Ty said, she had her good days and bad. From the smile on Ty's face, Tammy assumed she'd had a stretch of good ones.

"She's doing pretty good, thanks. Having Riley at the house for the whole weekend always does it for her."

"Your niece is the cutest thing going," Tammy said. "Is she excited to be a flower girl?"

"Oh, yeah," Cassie said. "And with Nick as her partner, I'm worried they'll steal the show."

Tammy grew quiet. The two kids were adorable, and barely annoying. She thought back to the herd of little Donatos that ran through her parents' place and had to admit they were pretty cute, too. There were just so many of them.

"Do you have your dress yet?" Cassie asked her.

Tammy raised her brows. "Mine? I'm only a guest, sweetie. Happily free of the planning and the worry that goes along with it."

"Did you help plan any of your sisters' weddings?" Claire asked.

Tammy shuddered dramatically. "All of them. I can't wait to get drunk at Cassie's bachelorette party and eat my weight in

Claire's pastries at the reception."

"And I'm looking forward to the bachelor party," Jake said with a wink.

Claire shot him a look but they all knew she had no worries there. The guy was devoted to his wife.

Ty rubbed his hands together. "So what do you guys have planned?"

"You guys?" Tammy repeated. "Is Rick helping you?"

"Nope," Ben said as he joined them. "I am."

Tammy kept her expression even as she turned to face him. He'd gone back to his room since she'd seen him, and now wore worn jeans and a cream Henley. The shirt hugged his body and she managed to keep her tongue in her mouth. A few of the buttons were unfastened and she caught a glimpse of the strong chest beneath that shirt.

"Hi," she said, her voice weak to her ears.

"Hey," he said in return. His eyes stared into hers for a long second and she wondered if he was thinking about their clinch in the cart. He finally broke contact and nodded to his family. "Hey, guys."

"Hi, Ben." Cassie buzzed a kiss on his cheek. "Please tell me you and Jake aren't going to ruin my groom for me."

"No ruining, Cassie." He grinned in Jake's direction. "Just a little bit of designed debauchery."

"Ha!" Jake laughed. "I like that, bro. And you're the guy to plan and design our night."

"Hmm, when is this night?" Claire asked.

The three guys exchanged a look, and then Ty shrugged. "I guess next Friday."

"Good," Cassie said. "You won't miss the rehearsal Thursday."

"Sweetheart, I wouldn't miss a thing," Ty said, brushing a thick lock of her hair behind her ear.

Her hair was the same shade of brown as Ben's. His looked so soft in the shaded lights of the tavern. He hadn't shaved for dinner, though. He still had that lovely stubble shadowing his face.

"Tammy?"

Claire's voice reached her and she dragged her gaze from Ben. She found her friend looking at her pointedly.

She blinked rapidly. "Hmm?"

"Are you coming?" Claire asked.

Tammy noticed then that everyone else had left the bar for the dining area. "Um, yes."

111

They were already sliding into seats at one of the large corner booths, since the round tables dotting the interior were too small for their party. The place was decorated much like an English pub, with dark wood panels and lots of greens and burgundies. It should have felt a little odd here in Florida but it worked, given the stuffy pretention available over in the Clubhouse. It was a nice counterpoint, and Tammy always recommended the place to prospective residents.

Ben stood as if waiting for her as the rest of them settled into their seats. He waved her in ahead of him and she briefly wondered at the wisdom of sitting so close to him. He would be pressed right up against her. That was unavoidable. But she would be facing Claire and Jake instead of him. Maybe that would help her get through this dinner she never should have agreed to.

When she sat and he followed, she knew it would take more than her friend's face to distract her from Ben.

***

Ben rubbed the back of his neck as he stood outside the tavern. Jake and Claire had already left for home, and Cassie and Ty were going to head out to their tent cabin at the far lakeshore.

"Good night, Ben." Cassie hugged him, giving him an extra

squeeze for good measure before pulling back. "It's fun, hanging out."

"It is," Ben admitted.

"So just call the Institute and set up a time you'd like an eco-tour," Ty put in.

"Will do."

The couple left, leaving him standing alone on the wide stone steps with Tammy.

"Well," he said. "That was fun."

Tammy gave him a small smile. "That so wasn't my doing, Ben. I promise."

"I never thought it was. I couldn't miss the grin on Claire's face."

"Yeah, she's up to something."

Ben could guess precisely what, but he wasn't going to point that out to Tammy.

He'd been squeezed in next to Tammy, her floral spice scent wrapping around him. His body obviously remembered what they'd almost done in the golf cart, though. He'd been half-hard since he saw her standing at the bar. A breeze kicked up, moving through her silky hair like it had on the cart. Damn, he couldn't seem to stop thinking about that tour. He stuffed his hands in his front pockets to keep from grabbing her right there on the steps.

"So, I guess I'll take off," she said.

"I'm parked over by the Sales Center," he said in lame answer.

"I'm walking, so good night."

"You're walking?"

"Yeah. I know I took the long way there when we were in the cart, but my townhouse is only a couple of blocks away."

"Let me drive you."

She nibbled on her bottom lip and he managed to keep from moaning. "I don't think that's a good idea."

"Why not?"

"Because if you drive me home I'm going to be very tempted to take advantage of you."

He threw his head back and laughed. "Ah, honey." He leveled a look at her. "You can't take what's freely given."

Her lips parted and he bent closer. Their mouths were a breath apart and he could already taste her.

"Ben," she whispered, her eyes staring deep into his.

Jerking away from her, he blew out a breath. "Sorry. Let me drive you home? I promise I'll stop at a goodnight kiss."

She gave an obviously reluctant nod. Was that reluctance

because she didn't want to agree or because she didn't want him to stop?

"'Kay," she said.

They reached his rental a little too soon but he held the door open for her.

She placed her hand on the doorframe and smiled. "More gentlemanly behavior, I take it?"

"Yep."

She slid into the seat and he watched her long, smooth legs for a second too long.

"Drive, sir," she said, a laugh in her voice.

He ducked his head to hide his smile and crossed to the driver's side. Starting the Jeep, he turned to her. "Where to?"

"Home, James," she teased. "Take a left at the stop sign and head toward the townhouses."

Ben nodded and they made their way. He'd seen this neighborhood before, of course. But there were a few townhouse and multi-family villages in Cypress. Once she directed him to take a left a couple of blocks from the Sales Center, he spotted her front porch.

He stopped and set the brake, turning in his seat as he left the engine running. "Here we are."

She stared at him for a long minute, and then leaned closer. He dropped his gaze to the V of her shirt. He could see her pretty purple bra and his mouth watered for another taste of her skin.

"How about that kiss?" she asked, coming closer.

He touched his lips to hers and felt himself sink into her. He got hard in an instant as she gave him her sweet tongue. He gripped her waist, longing to pull her closer even as he suspected he should go slowly. But when he deepened the kiss, her hands stole up to the nape of his neck and she sucked on his tongue. Damn, the girl could kiss.

His blood pounded low and thick as he took her into himself. Their bodies only touched fleetingly but he was primed for another brush of her form against his.

When she pulled back, her breath fast as she pressed her brow to his, he couldn't help but grin. She was as turned on as he was and just from one kiss. Okay, one phenomenal kiss.

"I have to go in," she said.

Her words gave him all sorts of ideas.

Ben growled softly. "Watch what you say, Tamara."

Her eyes opened and she smiled. Her lips were shiny and very pink and he nipped at her bottom lip with his teeth. Her fingers tightened in his hair before she released him.

"This isn't good." She snorted. "I mean, it's *really* good but we shouldn't do this."

"Why the hell not?"

"Look what happened this morning."

He moved his hands from her waist down to cup her fine ass. "Think what could happen tonight."

"That's what worries me," she said in a small voice.

She gazed at him, her hazel eyes very dark in the meager light from the streetlight. He knew the lights were dark-sky compliant, an eco-friendly fact he'd seen trumpeted all over the website and the Institute literature. That didn't matter right now, though. It was soft and gentle and caressed her smooth skin so well his fingers itched to touch her.

"Tammy, I promise the craziness that took over this morning won't show its face again."

"You can't make that promise." She touched him, her fingers caressing his jaw. "And neither can I."

Chapter 9

Ben kissed her again, and then turned off the engine with a jerk. "Let's get inside before I do something to shock the neighbors."

Tammy smiled and he knew in his gut that they were both in for something amazing tonight. She didn't wait for him to open her door. Nope. She took smooth, unhurried steps that he suspected were just for show. He'd seen the heat in her gaze. Tasted the need in her kiss.

He soon joined her on the front porch, barely able to keep from touching her a little bit as she unlocked her door. Then they were in her entryway but he barely noticed anything but the girl in front of him. She locked the front door and flicked the lights on.

He got the impression of a couch with fat cushions that he couldn't wait to try out. The fabric was crisp linen yet the lines weren't formal. No. The style was comfortable and chic.

"The place suits you," he said.

The pleased flush on her face told him she was proud of the home she'd made. "I like it." She kicked off her heels and began to unbutton her shirt, showing him more of that lacy purple bra he'd touched earlier today. Her breasts were held lovingly by that lace and his mouth watered. "Come on, Big Ben. Don't keep me waiting."

Desire slammed through him so hard his eyes nearly rolled back in his head. He kicked off his sneakers and started to lift his shirt over his head, and then stilled. "Wait." He looked around the living area, taking in the high ceilings and hardwood floors. "What are the specs on this townhouse?"

She clicked her tongue, draping her shirt over one of the stools near the tall counter bracketing the kitchen. "It has very thick walls, Mr. Architect. Fireproof." She came close to him and slid a hand over his belly up to his chest and he groaned. "And soundproof."

He closed his eyes as she teased him with her nimble hands. Lifting his arms, he let her push his shirt up and over his head to fall somewhere behind him. She brought her face up to his neck and gave him a lick. He looked down as she smiled up at him.

"Mmm. You're a beautiful man." She hooked her fingers in the waistband of his jeans, tugging him toward that very comfortable-looking couch. He let her take the lead, for the moment. His dick was hard as a rock and he caught her smile when she brushed her fingers over the front of him.

119

"You seem to be having the same trouble you had this morning," she said.

He hissed out a breath, and then grabbed her hand and brought it to his mouth. Licking her knuckles, he watched a blush spread over her light olive skin. "It couldn't be helped this morning, Tamara."

She let out a soft purr and began to unbutton his fly. "Tonight it can."

"Not yet." He drew her closer and kissed her, molding her to him as tightly as he could. "Damn, you taste so good."

She pushed him down on the couch and he sat, his legs spread. Reaching behind her, she unzipped her skirt and let it fall to the floor. She stepped out of it and straddled his lap, running her fingers through his hair. "I won't sleep with you, Ben."

He tried to concentrate on what she was saying, but need was seriously fogging his brain. He ran his hands over her back, and then down to her ass that fit perfectly in his hands. "Why not?"

"It's complicated." She arched against him and he buried his face in her cleavage. "Way too complicated."

"What's complicated?" He used his tongue to tease the edge of her bra. "Your reason?"

She laughed, shivering as she rubbed herself against his groin. "The situation, Ben."

He could barely think, but he knew she was blowing smoke. He could feel her heat through his jeans, for God's sake. She wanted this as much as he did.

"The situation is I want you." He nibbled on her skin and found her nipple through her bra. She moaned as it pebbled against his tongue. One touch to her pussy through the lace and he could tell she was wet. "And you want me."

"I do," she breathed. "But I don't do forever and you have forever written all over you."

He lifted his head, studying her graceful throat as she let her head fall back. He didn't want forever. He didn't even know what he wanted past the next six months. He couldn't admit that, though. She'd think he was just trying to get into her hot little purple panties. So he said nothing. He just slid his fingers deep inside her.

"Ben!"

She wriggled against him and he started the rhythm he knew would drive her over the edge. This was better than in the golf cart. Tonight he had her tight up against him with nearly nothing between them. Her scent was strong and sweet as she began to keen softly.

"Then what are we doing here, Tamara?"

"Oh, I love how you say my name!"

He bit down on her nipple. Hard. She came then, and he was very grateful the place was soundproof.

After she recovered, she leaned forward and pinned him with her passion-glazed eyes. "What are we doing? That's what you want to know?"

He could only nod, every nerve strung tight. She'd just come in his lap, for God's sake. It was a beautiful sight he wouldn't soon forget.

She shrugged. "Making each other a little bit happier. And remember, I'm driving."

With that, she slid down to kneel between his thighs. He watched as she deftly unbuttoned his fly and freed him. Her touch was magic and he sucked in a breath as he began to pound.

"Christ, Tammy."

She winked up at him. "Big Ben was a pretty good guess," she teased.

Then she took him in her mouth. He wasn't inexperienced. He'd had lots of women in this very same position. But Tammy had tricks he'd never experienced before.

Dropping his head on the back of the couch, he reached out to run his fingers through her hair as she gave him the best damn blowjob he'd ever had. Her lips, her tongue and teeth, drove him crazy until he couldn't hold back any longer.

He came so hard he couldn't breathe. And she didn't stop licking and sucking until she'd taken every bit of him. Gulping air, he finally raised his head to look at her. She was grinning up at him, her face flushed and her lips plump and wet.

"See, Ben?" She stacked her hands on his thigh, resting her cheek against them. "Happy."

"Happy? You nearly killed me, honey."

She shrugged, coming to her feet. He drank in the picture she made in her lacy underwear. Then he saw the serious expression on her face and thought back to what she'd said before she'd blown his mind.

"I have forever written all over me?" he asked.

Her lips turned down for a second, and then she shrugged again. "Yeah, you do. And it's a damn shame."

He sat up, tucking himself back in his jeans. "Why can't we just see where this goes?"

"You've asked me that before," she said. "It can't go anywhere."

She almost seemed afraid, her eyes wide, so he took his cue from her.

"Okay," he said. "Then why don't we see how happy we can make each other while I'm here?"

"Just a good time, Ben?" She picked up her skirt and stepped away from him. "Maybe. For a while, at least."

If he wasn't still reeling from when she'd turned him inside out, he might be offended that she expected him to hurt her. Instead, he forced himself to focus on what she'd just agreed to.

"So we can see each other?" he asked, needing clarification.

She clutched her skirt in her hands. "We're not dating, Ben. I'm not giving your family any ideas. And I'm not sleeping with you. No way."

"Then, what?" Did he even want to know?

She bit that full lower lip as she apparently thought her answer through. "Let's just keep this nice and easy. We're friends, right? That's what you said on Sunday."

"Friends." He stood, buttoning his fly. "Anything you say."

Was that disappointment in her eyes? He wasn't sure and he didn't want to press her. Instead, he grabbed his shirt up off the floor and put it on. He ran his fingers through his hair to keep himself from taking her in his arms and showing her just how happy he could make her right now.

"Good night, Tammy."

She gave a shaky nod. "Good night, Ben."

With that, he left and drove back to his room at the Cypress Inn. He should be happy as a pig in shit that she'd given him an out. She wasn't just an easy time. He knew that in his gut. He'd just think about the next time he could get her alone.

He'd show her just how happy he could make her.

***

Tammy stood there as if frozen. He'd left. Just like she'd wanted him to. "It's better this way," she told herself.

Oh, but when she took off his shirt she'd nearly lost her mind. He was so beautiful. Broad shoulders, strong arms, sculpted chest and abs, and a dusting of dark hair. She'd been on her knees too, and that gave her the perfect view of his stellar body. When he'd dropped his head back, his strong throat working as his abs tensed beneath her hands, she'd been tempted to climb back up on his lap and ride him into the sunset.

She'd kept her head, though. She'd given him pleasure and then gotten him the hell out of there. She couldn't sleep with him. Nope. She just wasn't ready for whatever he was bringing. He made her laugh. He made her melt. He gave her ideas she had no business thinking.

Sinking back down on the couch, she let out a long breath. She could still taste him. His kisses and more. He was dangerous. She'd known that from the first time she'd seen him in that hallway. God, had it only been last Friday? Jeez, it seemed like she was easier to make than a sandwich.

"Stop it," she said, getting up and gathering her clothes and shoes. "He's not for you." No matter how hot they both got each other.

By the morning, she was determined to put the craziness aside. She dressed as she always did. Pressed and polished with just a touch of sex appeal. It was her trademark, and part of what made her the best salesperson at Cypress. She wouldn't go to the coffee shop, either. No doubt Lettie would be there and she would pick up on just what happened, and didn't happen, last night. The woman was psychic. She would make her suspicions known to Tammy, too. There was no question about that. And if Lettie so much as mentioned Ben's name, Tammy suspected she'd blush head to toe. Wouldn't that be just peachy?

Claire was waiting for her when she got to her office, though. She was bright and sparkly and Tammy knew she was in for an interrogation.

"Good morning, Tammy," she practically sang.

"Good morning, Claire." Tammy turned on her laptop, feeling her friend's interest from behind. Unable to find an excuse to keep her from facing Claire, she turned and crossed her arms over her chest. "What?"

"Ben gave you a ride home."

That wasn't all he gave her. "So?"

"He's a Chapman, Tammy. He's nearly as hot as Jake and I know how tough that can be to resist."

"Who says I resisted?"

Claire's mouth dropped open. "You slept with him?"

Tammy shushed her and shut the door. "No, I didn't sleep with him. We just played around a little and I sent him home happy."

"Then what's the deal?"

"No deal. We're not seeing each other. We're not dating. And I'm definitely not going to sleep with him."

Claire shook her head, her brow furrowed. "Yeah, that's just what I said about Jake."

"Your situation is so different from mine, Claire."

Claire shrugged. "If you say so. Ben's working here now, you know."

"Today?" Tammy's pulse kicked. "I thought he didn't start until tomorrow."

"He doesn't. Jeez, what was that reaction about?"

Tammy ran her hands over her skirt. "Nothing, really. He's hot, like you said. We have a strong attraction. I'm not denying that. But he's not for me."

"Why not?"

"He's a Chapman, for God's sake," Tammy snapped. Claire winced and Tammy held up a hand. "Sorry. But you have to know what that means, Claire."

It was Claire's turn to cross her arms. "Please enlighten me."

"He's forever. I don't do forever."

"Look, I admit I don't know Ben very well. He seems like a good guy, but how do you know he's forever?"

"They all are."

Claire laughed softly. "Not at first, they're not. Believe me."

"Are you saying I should want the fairytale? Not my thing."

"Okay, okay. You seem to have your mind made up. You'll just keep him in the friend zone."

"I will. I mean, I'll try to anyway."

Claire opened her door. "Good luck with that. Jake and I

were there for about a week at the longest."

"We're not you and Jake. Not by a long shot."

"If you say so."

Tammy let out a little growl. "Oh, you're such a pain in my butt today."

Claire winked and sailed out of the office. Tammy walked to her door but by the time her hand hit the handle, Ollie popped his head in.

"Hey, hot stuff," he sang.

She stiffened. "Don't you start, either."

Ollie held up his hands. "What's got you all riled up?"

Tammy pressed her lips together and gave him a slow shake of her head.

"Let me guess." Ollie stepped in and propped a hip on the edge of her desk. "It starts with a Big and ends with a—"

"Shut up, Ollie," she bit out.

Ollie lost his smile and came closer. "Hey, what's wrong sweetie?"

Tammy covered her face with her hands as her eyes pricked with tears. Taking in a deep breath, she squared her shoulders and looked Ollie right in his pretty perfect face. "Nothing's wrong. I just had the same conversation with Claire and I don't have time for this right now."

Ollie didn't look like he believed her but she wasn't in the mood for more revelations this morning. She knew she wanted Ben. Hell, everyone knew she wanted Ben. It was clear he wanted her, at least to her. He kept up his laid-back Cali guy persona with everybody else. She'd seen him tense, though. Pushed to the limit. And she'd seen him so sated he'd nearly roared his satisfaction.

"Seriously, I have several tours scheduled this morning," she said, softening her tone.

Ollie appeared to be placated but she knew it wouldn't be for long. "Yeah. Me, too."

She waved him out of her office. "Then be gone. Before someone drops a house on you, too."

He barked out a laugh at the Wizard of Oz reference. "Hey, as a friend of Dorothy I have immunity."

She found a laugh and shooed him out the door anyway. "Go. We'll talk at lunch. I promise."

Ollie pouted. "About nothing good, I bet." Tammy just leveled a look at him and he laughed again. "Okay, I'm out of here. See you at lunch."

She gave a firm nod and he finally left her alone. Settling

into her chair, she stared out the window. She had a lovely view. Almost as nice as the one from Claire's office. The trees she could see were still full and green. The sun was bright, which wasn't a surprise in early September. Cassie and Ty's wedding was a week from Saturday, and the weather promised to be more of the same.

She was going to the wedding, of course. Ben would be there. He was the bride's brother. At least she wasn't in the party. She could get out of there as soon as things even looked like they were heating up between her and Ben. He'd be stuck there. Wouldn't he?

"I sure hope so," she murmured.

"What is that you're hoping for, Tammy?" Rick asked from the doorway.

Why hadn't she closed the damn thing when Ollie left? "A sale, boss. Always a sale."

Rick smiled. "There's our girl. Your tour is in the lobby, by the way."

Tammy looked the time on her laptop and stood. "A little bit early. Just how I like 'em."

Rick stepped back as she crossed to the doorway. "You had dinner with my brother last night?"

She froze, and then faced him. "Yep. Both your brothers and your sister, actually."

"That's what Cassie said."

So everyone was talking about this now? "It was fun. You have a great family, Rick."

His eyes brightened. "I know. I'm a lucky S-O-B."

Tammy just smiled at him and closed her office door. "Well, off to the races."

"Have at them, Tammy," Rick said in parting.

She pasted on her salesgirl smile and breezed into the lobby. Her ten o'clock group consisted of a family of five. This would be easy-peasy. Cypress was all about the family stuff and this bunch looked like they'd eat it up like Nona Donato's lasagna.

And if she looked for Ben around every corner of her tour this morning? That was just her too-bad.

Chapter 10

Ben decided he liked his sister's fiancé. The eco-tour was everything Ty had promised, along with glimpses of animals Ben had never seen back in Santa Cruz. Jesus, what the hell was a fox squirrel? Ty had an easy way with his explanations and Ben learned a lot.

"So algae is the new green, huh?" he asked Ty as they drove past the flatland designated for raceways, or algae ponds.

Ty smiled in that easy way he had. "I think it's always been green, Ben. But yeah, that would make the most sense if Cypress wants to start making its own energy. They have the land out this way. They'll probably use up to fifty acres. Although they're a few years away from starting construction on them. The Institute is researching companies to ultimately run the operation."

"Why not use the natural ponds?"

"They can't control it," Ty said. "The raceways are concrete and the water is constantly moved by paddlewheels."

"So it doesn't stagnate?"

"Yep." Ty turned the custom gator vehicle around and headed them back toward the town center.

Ben settled back in his seat, his mind working.

"Solar panels and bio-fuel," he said. "I have to tell you, I still can't believe a place like Cypress thinks to the future. I mean, exclusive villages, golf course and state-of-the-art homes? This is scratching me where I itch, man."

Ty dipped his head. "I'm excited to see what you have planned for the new neighborhood, Ben."

It was Ben turn to smile. "My mind's been working since Tammy took me out to see the place."

Of course, he wouldn't tell Ty that she figured prominently in thoughts that had absolutely nothing to do with sketches and plans.

"You start tomorrow, right?" Ty asked.

"Officially, yes. I'm looking forward to it."

"For what it's worth, I think this will be as good for you as it will be for Cypress."

Again, the prospect of putting down roots both tempted and terrified him. "For the time I'm here, I plan to make a difference."

"For the time you're here? You're not planning on going back to Boston, are you?"

"God, no. Chapman Financial is so not my scene."

"I couldn't imagine being stuck in that office all day," Ty

said. "How Rick and Jake did it for so long, I have no idea."

"I couldn't stand it."

"Then what's driving you away from Cypress? Nothing could get me to leave. Not on a bet."

"You have family here, Ty."

Ty glanced at him before eyeing the path ahead again. "You have family here, Ben. A whole bunch of it."

"True." Ben grew quiet for a minute. "I guess I'm not sure where I'm headed."

"Then give Cypress a chance, man."

Ben nodded. "I will. I couldn't have picked a prettier place to hang for a while."

"Right?"

They fell into a comfortable silence as the gator's nubby tires bounced over the rough terrain. This tour was very different from the sales tour Tammy had given him. That was for sure. The land and foliage looked almost foreign to Ben, but it was really beautiful in a wild way. Sort of like Tammy, when she finally let go of that salesgirl polish she usually wore.

He bit back a curse. He'd told her he wouldn't press for more. That he would take things nice and easy and dance to her tune. It was no hardship. He could keep himself pretty happy just getting her naked for a little while. She didn't want to sleep with him, though. He was damned if that didn't sting a little bit.

He thanked Ty when they got back to the town center and then he went right back to his room at the inn. He didn't want to risk running into Tammy. Not so soon after have his hands on her and her mouth on him. He didn't need to be sporting wood when his brother and sister-in-law were around.

"See you later, Ben," Ty said, crossing the street to the Institute.

Ben raised a hand and got into his Jeep. He was resigned to a lonely night in his room, which he would put to good use. He wanted to read up more on the algae fields Cypress planned. He'd also research materials for the eco-friendly homes he would soon be designing.

That jolt of creativity bit him hard. As he pulled the Jeep into the inn's parking lot, his cell jingled. A glance at the screen showed his father's number. The guy waited nearly a week to contact him. Must be a new record.

He swiped to answer the call as he got out of the car. "Hello."

"Ben." His father's voice was gruff, as usual. "How's it going?"

Ben nodded at the innkeeper as he entered the main parlor. "How's what going exactly?" he asked his father.

"Your new job."

Ben shook his head as he strolled out onto the patio overlooking the lakeshore. "I start tomorrow."

"Forbes told me. They're lucky to have you, son."

Ben stilled. "Thanks." He scanned the lakeshore, his eyes falling on the lounge chairs that were sadly empty. "I'm actually going to get started on a few plans tonight."

"Good, good. Hit the ground running. Like a Chapman."

Ben rolled his eyes. "Was there anything else you needed?"

"No."

There was silence on the line but Ben knew his father by now. The guy simply disconnected when he was finished with a conversation. He was lingering for some reason.

"Dad?"

Ben's use of the word seemed to snap Bill out of his trance.

"Uh, I wondered about your sister's wedding. Is everything all set?"

"I think so. I'm not a part of the planning process, thank God."

Bill laughed a little. "Yeah."

"Are you coming down?" Ben asked.

"I'm not sure."

"Look, I'll tell Cassie you called if you'd like."

"Yeah, do that. Please."

Please? Ben's mouth dropped open. Bill never begged for anything.

"If there's nothing else?" Ben prodded.

"No, no. Call me if you need anything."

Then his father disconnected as usual. That put Ben back on firmer footing. He stared at the screen and thumbed through his contacts. He found a bunch of Chapmans in there, which still surprised him. Tapping on his sister's name, he settled in one of the padded wicker chairs. Cassie answered before it rang twice.

"Hey, Ben!"

His heart clenched a little at the warmth and welcome in her voice. "Hey, Cassie."

"What's up?"

"I wanted to let you know that Bill called me."

She blew out a breath he almost felt. "He wants to come to the wedding."

"He didn't say as much but he asked how the plans were going."

"What do you think I should do?" she asked.

"About Bill?"

"Yeah, about Bill. Jake and Rick told me to tell him to fuck off but he's my father."

"What does Ty say?" Ben asked.

"Ty is a doll-man. He wants it to be my decision."

"Cassie, do you want him there?"

It grew silent on her end but he could hear her breath coming fast. "I do," she whispered.

"Really? Then that's your answer. He doesn't have to give you away, you know."

"I know." She sighed more loudly this time. "Rick is partnering Harmony and Jake is Ty's best man. Claire is my matron-of-honor. I have so few friends down here."

"What are you getting at?"

"I want you there, too."

"I'm planning on coming."

"But I mean really there, Ben. Not on the sidelines."

"What, you want me to be ring bearer? I think Nick would have a problem with that."

She laughed. "I want to make sure you have a good time at the wedding. Are you bringing anyone?"

"Who would I bring?" As if he didn't know who his sister was talking about. "I'm new to Cypress."

"Well, you could bring Tammy."

"I thought she was already coming."

"Oh, she is! I just want to make sure she has a good time, too."

Ben wanted to give Tammy a good time himself, but he couldn't tell his sister that. "Then I'll see her there, right?"

"I guess so."

"Then it's settled. Do you want me to call Bill for you?"

"No. I should do it," she said. "After I stop at the tavern for a couple of drinks."

Ben laughed. "Nah, Cassie. You're the strongest one of all of us. I hadn't known you five minutes before I saw that."

"Aw, you're a good big brother, Ben."

He was? "Thanks."

"I'll talk to you later," Cassie said.

"Later," Ben said, and they both disconnected.

He went back to staring out at the lakeshore. He had a father. He'd always known that. He had a sister and two brothers. That was newer information he was still processing. But after his call to Cassie? He realized something even more surprising.

He had a family. Pity was he still wasn't sure how he felt about that.

***

Tammy stretched her arms over her head, ready for this day to be over. Yesterday had been hopping with tours and presentations, but today Ben had started at Cypress. She kept hearing the sound of his voice. His deep, delicious voice that sent shivers through her. She caught sight of him now and then. He looked crisp, professional and hot as hell in his chinos and dress shirt and tie.

He'd eaten lunch with Rick at the tavern, a fact she'd overheard, and strolled around the displays in the Sales Center. He didn't come to her door, though. Or go out of his way to get in her space. That was what she wanted, right?

"Ready to call it, Tammy?" Ollie adjusted his messenger bag across his chest as he looked her over. "It's Wednesday."

"Yeah, Ollie." She shut off her computer and stood. "I'm just finishing up and then I'm dressing for class."

Ollie nodded, looking like he was holding back a smile.

She placed her hands on her hips. "What's up?"

He was all innocence now, his eyes wide and his brows

arched. "Nothing. See you tomorrow."

Putting Ollie's odd behavior out of her head, she grabbed her bag from her bottom drawer and headed to the ladies' room. She kicked off her heels and stripped, and then pulled on her fitted black capris. She zipped her favorite fuchsia sports bra, and then tied her sneakers. Scraping her hair back from her face, she fastened it in a high ponytail and scrubbed her face free of makeup.

It was a good thing she didn't have a tour right now. No-makeup Tammy might be a little hard to take. Smirking at herself in the wide mirror, she stuffed her work clothes and heels back in her bag and headed out to the breakroom to fill her water bottle.

Humming to herself, she rooted around in the fridge to find a bottle set near the back. A Zumba class outside in the square in September, even at six o'clock in the evening, could be very hot and humid as a mother. She grabbed an extra-cold bottle and straightened just as she heard a sound behind her. Glancing over her shoulder, she caught Ben watching her. His gaze was focused firmly on her butt and she laughed softly.

"Hey there, Big Ben." She closed the fridge and he brought his gaze to her face. "Cat got you tongue?"

He gave her a slow smile. "Do you know what you look like in that outfit?"

She nodded. "Yep, I do. And I work hard for it. Besides, it lets me move during class."

He blinked at her, still looking a little dazed and a whole lot turned on. "Class?"

"Yes, Ben. Zumba class."

When he didn't say anything she set her bottle on the counter and crossed her arms. "Zumba. Cardio and toning exercises set to peppy Latin music. Pitbull figures prominently."

"Oh." He swallowed audibly. "You take a Zumba class."

"I lead a Zumba class. On Wednesdays. In the town square." She glanced at the clock on the microwave. "In about ten minutes."

His eyes grew wide. "You're going to be jumping around the town square wearing that?"

She placed a hand on her hip and struck a pose. "Is there a problem, Mr. Chapman?"

"A seemingly endless supply of them."

His eyes ran over her again and she felt herself grow hot in a rush. Her nipples pressed tight against her sports bra and she sucked in a breath.

143

"So Zumba," he said. "That's how you get that body. By working hard."

She managed to hold onto her composure at his double-entendre. "Yeah. But not just Zumba. How do you keep that fine body of yours in shape?"

"I run. Strength-train." He eyed her again. "I haven't seen you out on the trails."

"I don't run. I do use the Fitness Center."

He arched a brow. "I haven't seen you in the gym."

"Ugh, never the gym. I prefer hot yoga."

He closed his eyes as his lips moved in what she guessed was a silent prayer. "Hot yoga?"

"It's steamy. Sultry." His pupils dilated and she couldn't resist teasing him a little bit more. "Bending. Stretching. Lots of different positions."

"Christ," he rasped.

Ooh, his voice did things to her. Hoping she looked more cool and collected than she felt, she rifled through her back unnecessarily and zipped it shut. She turned back to the counter to fill her bottle with the water from the fridge and felt him step very close behind her.

"Do you know how much I want to unzip that sexy little bra

and show you just what particular problem I'm having right now?"

Her hand shook and she spilled some water on the counter. She could feel him now. His sculpted chest against her back, his strong thighs against hers and his hard "problem" against her butt.

She deliberately put down the water bottle and leaned herself closer to the counter, gripping the edge. "Not going to happen, friend."

"Friend." He laughed in her ear, his breath fanning over her neck. "Okay, then."

When he stepped back, relief swept over her. Along with a touch of disappointment. That was a very impressive problem he had there, and she was on a first-name basis with it after Monday night.

She returned her attention to her bottle and managed to fill it without any more spillage. "Look, Ben." She closed the top and wiped up the spill before turning to face him. "We talked about this. You know just where the aforementioned unzipping would lead."

He looked her over, nice and slow, as his eyes grew dark. "Yeah. I do."

"And we agreed that wasn't in the cards."

He shrugged. "Yeah. We did."

The air crackled between them and her heart was racing like she'd just danced around the square for an hour and a half. Placing her hand on his chest, his very nice chest, she gently pushed at him.

"I have a class to get to."

Ben stepped back, waving at the doorway. "Have a good class."

She shouldered her bag and grabbed her bottle, taking a nice, long drink. "Thanks."

She left him there, probably staring at her butt again. Her body tingled everywhere they'd touched. And a few places they hadn't.

"Channel the energy into class, Tammy," she told herself.

She headed out to the square to start the class, hoping that the pounding music and demonstrating the repetitive dance steps would keep her mind from Ben and what might have happened if she hadn't gotten out of there.

Chapter 11

The next morning Ben was still reeling from drinking in the sight of Tammy in her workout clothes. He'd never seen anything hotter. Yeah, he'd seen in her in underwear but those clinging black pants made her legs look strong and long and that dark pink zippered bra? A zippered bra! Damn, he'd wanted to free those gorgeous breasts of hers a millimeter at a time until they spilled into his waiting hands. Against his eager mouth.

All night he'd replayed their all-too-brief contact against the counter in his head, too. The scenario he'd envisioned ended a lot differently than with him cooling his heels, and his dick, alone in the breakroom. No. In his mind, he'd peeled those tight pants off her legs slowly. He'd grabbed her and sat her on the counter so he could lean in closer. He'd licked and nibbled her all over until he—

"Good morning," Claire sang as she entered the Sales Center a step or two behind him.

"Hey, Claire." His voice was a little rough.

She smiled at him. "I didn't get to ask you yesterday. How did your first day go?"

"Good, thanks."

Claire nodded. "I'll see you around the place, then."

He nodded, and then stood like an idiot in the lobby, waiting for Tammy to show up. After what he'd just been thinking, he couldn't imagine how he would react when he saw her in the delectable flesh. He had to make himself scarce and fast.

He headed toward Mr. Forbes' office and rapped on the door. He knew the guy already, and Forbes was as likely to show up early as anybody else. As expected, Forbes called out for him to enter.

"Good morning, Mr. Forbes," Ben said.

"'Morning, Ben." He patted a stack of papers on his neat-as-a-pin desktop. "I'm looking forward to seeing some of your plans."

"And I'm eager to show them to you. I have a few preliminary sketches but I have to get more feedback on just how green we want these homes."

Forbes nodded, his brows drawn together. "Hmm. Have you contacted the Institute yet?"

Ben nodded. "I went on an eco-tour with Ty on Tuesday."

"That's a great start." He scratched his chin. "You know, why don't you get with Jessie? She's sort of our go-between for the Sales Center and the Institute."

"Jessie?" He hadn't met anyone named Jessie, or at least he didn't remember meeting her.

"She works at the Institute on Wednesdays. Have Tammy introduce you two this morning."

Ben nodded even as he thought it might be a little bit dangerous to approach Tammy after his fantasies of last night.

"Will do," he told his boss.

Forbes nodded again. "Good."

Ben knew a dismissal when he heard one, but this one didn't feel abrupt like his father's usual M.O. He gave Forbes a two-fingered salute and closed the guy's door behind him. And ran right into Tammy.

She bumped up against him just for a split second but it was enough to set his pulse pounding.

"Ben!"

"Good morning, Tammy." He forced himself to step back. "I actually wanted to get with you this morning."

She arched one brow. "I'll just bet."

He chuckled. "Not touching that one. Seriously, I wondered if you could introduce me to Jessie?"

"Jessie?" Her face brightened. "Oh, yes! She's just perfect for you."

149

It was his turn to arch a brow. She waved a hand at him.

"She's as eco-minded as Ty, and that translates very well to the sales side of things. Come with me."

She ducked into a large office he'd only seen in passing and he noticed it held several desks. Ollie lifted a hand in greeting as he continued his phone call. A desk was unoccupied but there was a young woman seated at another one. She was a little thing, with short blond hair and a pixie face. She reminded him of Tinkerbell. She wore a cardigan that was twice the size she was.

"Hey, Jessie," Tammy called.

The woman turned, blinking up at them. "Good morning, Tammy." Her big eyes went wider as she spied him, her cheeks going pink.

They walked closer to her. "This is Ben Chapman. You know he's designing the new neighborhood."

Jessie's mouth dropped open. "This is just great. Another one."

Her words were soft but Ben caught them. And so, apparently, did Tammy. She laughed softly and shook her head.

"Ben here needs your input on the promotional material," Tammy went on. "He's going to get with the Institute soon."

Jessie's face lit up. "Oh, Dr. Robbins will gladly give you

any info you need. Have you taken a tour with Ty yet?"

"Tuesday."

"Good." She stood, running her hands over her slightly-wrinkled skirt.

"I'll leave you to it, then." Tammy winked at Ben, which sent another jolt through him, and left him to Jessie's care.

Grabbing up a pair of glasses set on her desktop, she set them on her little nose and thumbed through the stack of brochures in a clear plastic holder on her desk. "I have some maps here. Trails and things." She shoved three glossy brochures into his hands. "Here's one on identifying wildlife." Ben caught another brochure. "Hmm." She perched back in her seat and pulled open one drawer. "I have a prospectus on biofuel, if you're interested."

"I am, but not right now." He smiled and waved the handful of literature she'd already given him. "I'll look these over. Thanks, Jessie."

She beamed a smile at him and he realized she was a cute little thing. "Sure thing, Ben."

Her shyness seemed to come back as she ran out of things to hand him. He thanked her again and left, passing Ollie's desk as he did so.

"Another one falls under your spell, Big Ben?" he asked.

Ben just shook his head. "Shut up, Ollie."

The guy laughed out loud. "You sound just like Tammy."

That made Ben smile. He slowed his pace as he neared Tammy's office but the door was closed tight. He continued down to his brand-spankin'-new office and placed the literature down on his desk. There was a drafting table set near the wide window, and he ran his hand over the smooth, slanted top. This was what he was meant to do. Draw. Create.

He stared out the window, looking out at the trees and green spaces. Cypress was a pretty great place. He had a job he could really love. He had family who seemed to like having him around. He should be so happy right now he should be whistling. Yet something was niggling at him.

It was like at any moment it could all go south again. Be left all alone, like after his mother died. She'd been sick but, sweet flower child that she'd been, she'd leaned on the belief that a stress-free life and healthy eating would cure her of breast cancer where medicine would only make her sicker. He'd insisted and she'd proved him right, in a way. Her first round of chemotherapy had dragged her down and taken away her spark. He'd relented and bit back his disagreement when she'd decided to forego more treatments. She'd died six months later.

His creativity had grown as dry as dust, and he'd tried hard to rekindle his own spark. At times he felt like he could lose it all. Maybe he was just borrowing trouble.

He thought about Tammy and smiled ruefully to himself.

Or maybe he just needed to get laid.

***

Tammy put a coffee pod in the machine, needing the pickup after a hectic morning. She'd had back-to-back tours, which was good since it kept her focused on the job and not on the guy. Oh, he looked good today. Seriously, he looked good every day this past week but there was something about pressed and neat Ben that made her want to mess him up.

"Mmm, that smells good," Jessie said as she came into the breakroom. "Pop one in for me?"

"Sure." She put a clean cup on the stand and pressed the button. She fixed her own coffee as Jessie's brewed, turning to face her as she stirred her cup. "So. What's new?"

Jessie flushed pink, just like Tammy knew she would. Jessie was a good salesperson and a doll of a girl, but Tammy got a kick out of her shyness. Jessie blushed even easier than Claire did.

"Oh, it's too much some times," Jessie said, picking up her own cup. "Don't you think it's too much?"

Tammy sat at the closest table, leaning her elbows on the surface as she sipped her coffee. "Exactly what is too much, Jessie?"

Jessie rolled her eyes and sat down across from her. "The guys around here. Each one is hotter than the next! It's just too much."

"Actually, I don't think it's enough," Ollie quipped as he joined them.

Tammy grinned at him. "Sorry to say, but every last one of them plays on our team."

Jessie snorted a laugh and Tammy nodded to her.

"Sad but true." Ollie folded his arms on the table. "Wait until you guys get a load of the new guy."

"Ben?" Jessie's voice sounded a little dreamy. "I saw him this morning."

Ollie gave a slow shake of his head. "Nuh uh. Not Ben."

Jessie let out a little whimper. "Are you freaking kidding me?"

"What new guy, Ollie?" Tammy asked.

"There's a new builder coming on as a partner," Ollie said.

"I heard the name of the company and I looked him up."

"You looked him up," Tammy repeated. "Do tell."

"The builder is a hottie. That's all I'm saying."

Tammy leaned forward. "When does the new builder start? Do we have any info for our tours?"

Ollie shook his head. "That's not the line of questioning I would have expected from you in the past, girlfriend."

Tammy waved a hand. "Never mind. You know I'm all about the job."

"That's true, Ollie," Jessie piped in. "The guys fall all over Tammy but she stays focused."

Tammy raised her brows. "They fall all over me? Pray, tell me where I am when all this falling happens?"

Jessie smirked, which was an adorable expression on the pixie. "Just look at Ben Chapman."

At the mention of Ben's name, Tammy's face grew hot. She suspected she was as pink as Jessie had just been.

"Yes, please," Ollie said. "Let's look at Ben Chapman."

Jessie placed her hand over her heart. "Those pretty blue-gray eyes of his strayed to Tammy again and again."

Tammy studied the inside of her coffee cup. "That's not true."

"But it is!" Jessie said. "If a guy ever looked at me like that?" She shivered. "I'd be a puddle on the floor."

Ollie nodded sagely. "Yep." He turned to face Tammy. "Speaking of puddles on the floor, what happened when Ben saw you all dressed for Zumba?"

Jessie's mouth was an O as she swung back around to gape at Tammy. "He saw you dressed for Zumba? Well, that's it then."

Tammy rolled her eyes. "Do I even want to know what that means?"

"He's seen you in those clothes, Tammy." Jessie leaned closer. "Those legs. That butt." She gestured at her own chest. "The ladies. Come on."

He'd also seen her with almost no clothes, but Tammy wasn't about to admit that aloud. "And?"

Jessie crossed her arms, lifting her chin. "There you go. He's smitten. He has to be."

Ollie grinned. "Hell, she almost tempts me to revert when I see her like that."

Tammy laughed out loud. "Ollie, you're so full of it!"

"I am," Ollie said. "Still. I bet Big Ben took a good, *hard* look."

Tammy shot a glance at the doorway, relieved no one was around to hear that little tidbit. She had to put a stop to this conversation, though. "Okay, I think playtime is over."

"You're right." Jessie drained her cup and popped out of her seat. "I have a tour at four o'clock."

She hurried out of the breakroom and Ollie hooked a thumb in the direction she took. "That pixie can fly."

Tammy smiled. "She's quick. And in more ways than one."

Ollie arched a perfectly-groomed brow. "Oh?"

Tammy clicked her tongue. "Not that way. She's only been here since May, but she's really finding her niche. She's got the nature thing down."

"Better her than me," Ollie said. "I'd rather talk about the Fitness Center."

"That's because it's gay church," Tammy teased.

"True!"

Tammy got up and brought her empty cup to the sink.

"So, girlfriend," Ollie went on. "Tell me what really happened when Big Ben got a look at you in all that spandex."

Tammy closed her eyes and thought about that moment when Ben had pressed hard against her from behind. Oh, he was so hot she'd practically caught fire. Fixing a serene look on her

157

face, she turned back to him. "We're friends, Ollie."

Ollie stood. "I can't listen to the party line again, sister. I'm not buying it. Besides, I have a tour waiting for me, too. You should have seen one of the guys. Sporting a belly bag and a backpack, for God's sake."

"Both?" Tammy laughed. "You're not going to say anything."

Ollie held up his hands. "Hey, there's nothing like a man with extra storage capacity. Makes you wonder what he's packing."

He winked at her and left. She should just give up. It was obvious to Jessie that Ben wanted her. It was clear to Ollie that Tammy wanted Ben right back. It was only a matter of time before she threw all of her conviction right out the window and climbed all over him right in the middle of the lobby!

Oh, how she wanted to be with him. Just that taste of him last Monday night had fueled her dreams, both asleep and awake. It was so wrong, though. For so many reasons. Gossip and rumors, aside, she didn't want to give his family any ideas. *It was so right, too,* her mind whispered.

She covered her face with her hands. "What am I going to do?"

"Can I make a suggestion?" Ben asked, his voice low.

Her head shot up and she found him staring at her. A smile teased his lips and she wanted to kiss it off his face.

"Please," she breathed.

She wasn't even sure what she was asking him, but apparently he didn't need any clarification at the moment.

"Ah, Tamara." His smile widened and his dimple came into view. "Just say when."

Chapter 12

Ben could hardly wait the hour until the end of the business day. He'd nearly leapt on Tammy when she'd breathlessly begged him for...something. He had to tread carefully, though. She was so afraid of any kind of commitment, not that he was offering her anything more than a good time while he was in Cypress.

He looked over the presentation he was putting together for the new project and frowned. He could be in Cypress for some time. Was it really fair to use their attraction for the unforeseeable future?

"Yes, damn it." He pushed away from his desk. "She wants me and I sure as hell want her."

It had to be tonight. Tomorrow was Ty's bachelor party and then the wedding would take up most of the weekend. He'd take Tammy to dinner and then back to his room. That was the civilized thing to do. It was completely beside the point that he wanted to grab her and take her any way he could, as many times as he could manage without killing himself.

Mentally giving himself a shake, he returned his attention to the presentation. It wasn't a formal one, but he was meeting with the director of the Institute next week and wanted to have something to show him. After reading through the brochures Jessie had given him, he was a little more familiar with the Institute's slant. There was still the bottom line to consider, and working in the Sales Center would help him keep a check on the pulse of the typical visitor. Prospective residents were his target. Not Chapman's investors, despite Bill's insistence to the contrary. He'd brushed off his father's intrusive questions in his phone call just yesterday.

He'd already begun preliminary drawings of several homes. One was a bungalow style a bit larger than the one Claire and Jake lived in. It was his favorite, since a lot of older homes in Santa Cruz were in the Craftsman style as well. He would design several large homes, too. This particular project would have lots and homes of varying sizes to accommodate a variety of homebuyers who had their eyes on the environment.

He stood and crossed to the draft table again. The bungalow design really called to him. Going back as far as he could remember, he'd lived in one with his mother until he'd finished his undergrad. Bill had bought the house and put money toward any renovations, which Ben had done himself. He put a lot of his sweat and heart into that house, but after his mother died he couldn't bear the thought of moving back in there. Instead, he'd kept to the apartment closer to Monterey Bay that he'd taken when he'd started his Master's years earlier. That was, until Bill contacted him with more than a job offer. He dumped the apartment and now he had no ties left in California.

Tracing the lines he'd put to paper, the organic way he preferred to start a project, he could almost imagine the family that would reside there. The home had four bedrooms, three upstairs, so no doubt a couple of kids would fill the space with laughter and tears. He thought about his nephew Nick, and wondered if his brother and Harmony would have another child soon. More family to call his.

A chef's kitchen and master suite at the back would please the husband and wife. An image suddenly filled his head. Tammy and him cuddling on the big couch, of course they would have a big couch, while a fantastic Italian dish sizzled in the kitchen.

He pulled his hand away as if the paper burned him. What the hell was he doing, thinking all domestic? It wasn't what Tammy wanted and it sure as hell wasn't what he wanted, either.

"Just fuck and forget, man," he told himself.

It was what he'd always done in the past. And he'd never

had any complaints, since the women he'd been involved with were of the same mind. Of course, his creativity left him at about the time he'd stopped taking women up on their offers of mutual gratification. Was there a connection there? Maybe.

He sat back down in front of his laptop and began to close the drafting program. The clock read five twenty-five, so he went ahead and shut the whole thing down. His body was humming now, primed for the slightest provocation.

A knock came at the door and he stood, rubbing his hands over his thighs. "Come in."

The door opened and Tammy stood there. He nearly lost his breath. Yeah, she was dressed professionally and her clothes fit snugly in all the right places as usual. But the expression on her face was what did him in. Her lips were curved in a slight smile and her gaze was hot on him.

"When," she said.

He must have heard her wrong. He had to know. He crossed to her, stopping a hairsbreadth away, and caught her scent. "You're sure."

It wasn't a question and she didn't really have to answer. It was clear in her hazel eyes.

"I prefer if everyone didn't know about this," she said.

163

This? God, that could mean anything and he couldn't wait to find out what. He stopped himself from grabbing her and doing her on his desk, but just barely.

"Let's grab something to eat," he said.

She leaned against the jamb, putting scant distance between them. "Why?"

"Ah, Tamara." He brought his face to hers. "You're going to need your strength."

They walked over to the tavern together, not touching but very close to, and he ordered a pizza to go. As they were waiting, his sister came in.

"Hey, Ben. Tammy." She looked from one to the other, her brow slightly furrowed. "What's up?"

"Getting a pizza," Tammy said.

Cassie lifted her chin at Ben. "You, too?"

He just nodded. Making sure no part of his body was touching Tammy's, he leaned an elbow on the take-out counter. "What's up with you?"

Cassie beamed a smile and suddenly hugged him, surprising the hell out of him. After a beat, he returned the hug.

She stepped back, that smile still on her face. "I called Bill."

"You did?" Tammy asked.

Ben crossed his arms. "How did that go?"

"Not too bad, actually." Cassie caught the attention of the young guy working the counter. "Picking up an order for Ty Walsh." The kid nodded and she turned back to them. "He's coming down tomorrow night. I got him a room at the Cypress Inn."

His brows raised. "Seriously?"

"Yeah," Cassie said. "Why?"

Tammy was hiding a smile, and he could just guess what she was thinking. Let her laugh if she wanted to. It didn't matter. There was no way in hell he would let his father put a damper on his plans for Tammy this weekend.

"Is he going to the bachelor party?" he asked his sister.

Cassie shook her head. "There's no way Jake and Rick want him hanging around during all that debauchery."

Ben nodded. "Neither do I." And at Cassie's pointed glare, he held up a hand. "Not that there will be any debauchery."

The guy brought out Cassie's order. She paid and then faced them again. "Thanks again, Ben. I don't think I would have ever called him if I hadn't talked to you."

Ben was without words, but smiled as he accepted the punch to his arm like the one he always saw her give Jake.

165

"Bye, Cassie."

She waved to Tammy too, and then it was just the two of them again.

"That was close," Tammy said.

"I'm not the one who wants to keep a lid on this," he pointed out.

She shrugged a shoulder. "What are you going to do with your father staying at the inn. All cramping your style?"

"Not gonna let it happen."

She moved a little bit closer. "He won't be here tonight."

Before he could find an answer to that, the guy brought out their pizza. He took the much-needed distraction and paid so they could get the hell out of there.

"Let's go," he said, holding the pizza box with one hand and pressing the small of her back with the other.

"In a hurry, Big Ben?"

He let her see the desire in his eyes for a second. "You have no idea."

***

Tammy's skin sizzled where he innocently touched her. There was nothing innocent about his words or the want clear on his face, though. How he'd hidden it from his sister, she had no idea. Cassie clearly had a lot on her mind with the wedding and her father's imminent arrival. If she'd looked closely at the two of them, she certainly would have seen the electricity sparking between them.

He held the door of his Jeep open for her and she got in, taking the pizza box from him. It smelled heavenly, all garlic and spice and tomatoes. A little like home. That caused a pang in her belly. Since when did she get home sick?

"So how do you like your room at the inn?" she asked, wanting desperately to fill the space with any words but the ones she wanted to say to him. *Kiss me. Take me. Love me.* She wouldn't say any of those, though. Well, maybe the first two. She'd sworn to herself she wouldn't sleep with him, so the second two were out. As for the third? No way would she utter those words she'd never said before in her life.

"You've never stayed there?" he asked.

She shook her head. "I moved into my townhouse right after I started here. Seems I bought what I was selling."

"I think you'll like it." He smiled. "Nice, big bed."

She shifted in her seat. "I'm not sleeping over."

He shrugged a shoulder. "I'm not asking."

That was all he said on the subject. Not asking? What did

that mean? Was he telling? God, she'd never been so off-balance with a guy. So out of control.

She liked being in control. Calling the shots. Any guy she'd been with? They'd usually both made their intentions clear to each other from the beginning, not that much time passed between the beginning and the end.

Before long, they reached the big, gorgeous B and B. He parked and turned to face her, one brow arched. She just looked at him, not hiding a thing. Why pretend she didn't want to get tangled up with him again?

He must have seen it, because his eyes grew dark. "Damn," he said, his voice low.

They were soon in his room, which was a very pretty place. She set the pizza down on the small table set near a tiny fireplace done in gray tile. The room didn't have the same Old Florida style as the exterior or the lobby and common rooms. It was furnished like a fine hotel. Ambient lighting. Clean lines. Sleek furniture. A big spa-like bathroom she could see through a doorway just beyond the enormous bed piled with pillows. The pillow top on the bed must be five inches thick. She couldn't wait to stretch out on it with the softness beneath her and Ben on top of her.

"You weren't kidding about the bed."

"Really big tub, too." Opening the small fridge, he turned to her. "Beer or wine?"

"Out of the minibar? Really, Ben. Such extravagance."

He chuckled. "No expenses spared, honey."

"Wine, then." When he handed her a tiny, single-serving bottle, she twisted off the cap and toasted him with it. "To my host."

He grabbed himself a beer and did likewise. "To my…*friend*."

Oh, how could he make that innocent word sound so naughty? They sat at the table and began to eat. She nibbled at her slice of pizza but he ate like a guy. Just watching him bite, chew and swallow got her thinking all sorts of things. She drank her wine down. She had to get on more sure footing and fast. She was in real danger of throwing herself at him. At that big bed. At a future she knew didn't exist but was starting to crave anyway.

Setting her empty bottle on the table, she leaned back and kicked off her shoes. "When, Ben."

He nearly spit out his beer, but apparently soon recovered. A slow smile spread across his face. "Now, Tamara."

169

Before she knew it, they were both tangled up on that bed and it was as comfortable as it looked. Ben was as hard as she'd imagined, too. The contrast was delicious as he pressed his body to hers, lifting himself onto an arm only long enough to remove and discard one article of her clothing after another. She was in her bra and panties when she finally held a hand against his chest.

"What?" he rasped. His hair was mussed and his eyes a little clouded. He looked adorably horny and a little confused.

She pushed herself up on her elbows and lifted one hand, making a swirling motion with it. "Clothes off."

He grinned, and then stood at the side of the bed and stripped like his clothes were on fire. *Whoa.* His legs were long and strong-looking. His chest was sculpted and his abs were perfection. His arms were defined. Was there a better sight in the world than a hot, fit guy in boxer briefs? She didn't think so.

It was clear through that thin layer of cotton that he was in a bad way. Good. That she could fix. The rest of it? Her feelings and the confusing way he made her feel? She'd just leave those over on the table with her empty bottle of wine and the nearly-empty pizza box.

Crooking her finger at him now, she sighed as he covered

her again. His skin was hot on hers. His every muscle tense as he rubbed his chest against her breasts. Her nipples tightened in an instant, her body arching of its own accord to gain more contact.

He kissed her, giving her his tongue. She took it, kissing him back just as ravenously. Slanting his mouth over hers, he took what she gave him as his hands began their magic. He'd pleased her twice before with those clever fingers. When her bra was gone he put them to amazing use on her flesh.

"God, you're gorgeous," he said, pinching and teasing her nipples.

He lowered his head and sucked on her. Hot pleasure shot through her. His teeth were sharp on her flesh and his hands began to wander again. She spread her legs to him, needing his hands on her.

"Touch me, Ben," she breathed.

He gave her nipple a long lick, and lifted his head. "I'll touch you, honey." He moved downward, his tongue stroking over her belly. "And taste you."

Her pulse spiked as he said the words, and then shot to the moon when he began to kiss her there. His tongue was as gifted as his hands, and with every lick he sent her higher until she couldn't hold on any longer. Arching again, she cried out as she

171

climaxed.

Breathing fast, she held a hand to her chest as she tried to collect herself. It was nearly impossible with this man. The bed felt like it was spinning.

He dropped a kiss on her navel. "I love to watch you come."

"What can I say?" She took in a breath. "You're good at what you do."

He laughed, a rumble against her belly. Pushing up on his hands, he covered her again. The cotton of his briefs rubbed against her still-swollen center and she bit her lip to keep back a moan of need. She wouldn't sleep with him. She couldn't sleep with him.

"Ben, you're making me want things I can't have," she admitted on a sigh.

"You can have it, Tammy." He growled softly as he ground tighter against her. "Take it."

She squeezed her eyes shut and shook her head. "No. Not fair."

"Fair?" He kissed her neck, causing tingles to course through her. "Seems fair to me. I want you." He fit himself against her and she gasped as she imagined how amazing they would be together. "You want me."

She shook her head again, opening her eyes to stare into his. "No." She gently pushed at his chest again. "On your back, Big Ben."

After a second he rolled over, obviously happy to accommodate her. She stretched out on top of him, managing to keep her traitorous lady-parts away from the part of him they craved. Instead she kissed him, memorizing his taste and catching hers on her tongue as well. His arms were strong around her and she leaned up on her hands to stare down at him.

"I haven't even known you two weeks," she stated.

It didn't really matter, but she figured it bore mentioning.

He shrugged, running his fingers through her hair as he smiled at her. "And yet, I've made you come three times."

She couldn't let him win that one. Cupping his erection, she smirked as he groaned loud and long. "Then I have no choice but to try and catch up."

He blinked, and then closed his eyes as she snuck her hand beneath the waistband of his briefs. "Tammy…"

She didn't answer him. Instead she bent her head, and gave him just what he'd given her. It was all she would allow herself. It would be enough for him. He was a guy.

It would just have to be enough for her, too.

Chapter 13

Friday morning, Ben was whistling as he entered the Sales Center. Tammy had driven him crazy last night. Her lips. Her tongue. And as she'd gone down on him he'd grabbed her and shifted on the bed so he could get another taste. He'd never come so hard. The memory made him hum.

The girl was amazing, even if she insisted on keeping her promise. She didn't stay over and she didn't let him close the deal. He'd grabbed her cell phone while she was in the very nice, spa-like bathroom he hadn't gotten to share with her. Put his number right in her contacts. Just in case.

Claire peeked her head out of her office as he passed, her face pink.

"Ben! Thank God."

"What's the matter?"

She stepped into the hallway. "Can you do me a favor?"

Ben nodded. "Sure. What do you need?"

"Those darn cake layers should be done by now."

He held up his hands. "Whoa, don't ask me to bake."

She blinked, and then laughed. "I'm not! The layers are in my oven and I need to take them out. I'm stuck waiting for this darn program to finish running so I can get the mid-month figures to Mr. Forbes."

"So you want me to go take them out of the oven?"

"I wouldn't ask, but Jake has a bunch of guys in to test the new apparatus."

"No worries. I'm happy to help."

She smiled and pressed her keys into his hand. "Just take them out and put them on the racks to cool."

"Racks?"

She stared at him for beat, and then nodded. "The racks, Ben. Wire racks. For cooling off things you bake?"

"You have to forgive Ben, Claire." Tammy walked up behind him, brushing her hip against his ass. "He's not well-versed in the kitchen like you and me."

"Go and show him?" Claire asked.

Ben felt her stiffen and step back. "I'm sure he can figure it out."

Ben slowly shook his head. "I don't know. I'm pretty clueless in the kitchen. I'd hate like hell to ruin Cassie's wedding cake."

Tammy snorted. "Fine. Let's go."

"Yes, hurry!" Claire said. "I don't want them to burn."

Ben waved Tammy ahead of him, hiding his smile. "Speaking of hot," he whispered in her ear.

She clicked her tongue. "Smooth-talker."

They got into Ben's Jeep and headed over to Jake and Claire's house. As he drove, he checked out Tammy's legs in her short-yet-professional skirt.

"I missed you last night," he said.

"Nuh uh," she said. "You can't miss me if I've never stayed over. And I'm never staying over."

"So you said."

"Why do I feel like you're not taking this seriously?"

"Oh, I'm dead serious honey. I'm going to get you in my bed for the whole night. Which we'll need, by the way."

She shuddered just slightly but he caught it. "Just drive, Casanova."

Chuckling, he pulled up to the house and the two of them went inside. He sniffed and let out a whistle.

"This place smells like the inside of a chocolate cookie," he said.

"Yep." Tammy hurried into the kitchen and headed for the wall oven. "Whew. Just about three minutes to spare."

He stepped closer, peering into the oven window. There

were several pans sitting on the racks. "I don't get it. The wedding isn't until tomorrow."

"The layers have to chill before she can ice them."

"I guess that makes sense."

She looked at the timer again, and then leaned back against the counter. "I take it you don't do much in the kitchen."

He laughed low at that. "I could."

She shook her head. "That's not what I meant."

"I enjoy designing them but no, I don't cook much. And I've never baked."

She stared at him. "Seriously?"

"My mother used to bake all the time." He shrugged. "I guess I never had to learn, so I never did. Got to lick the spoon, though." He winked. "Still do."

She laughed. "No naughtiness in your brother's house."

"Then come over tonight."

"Nope. The bachelorette party is tonight. And don't you have cigars and strippers awaiting you?"

"I doubt there'll be strippers. Cigars, yeah. We're hanging out at the tent-cabin."

"Have you ever been out there before?"

"No. Ty pointed it out when he took me on the tour

Tuesday." He thought for a second. Both of his brothers had a history with that little house-thing. Did they have a history with Tammy, too? "Have you?"

Her eyes narrowed. "What exactly are you asking me, Ben? Did I fool around with your brothers in Ty and Cassie's love shack?"

He held up his hands. "I wasn't asking."

"Yeah. You were." She crossed her arms, her brows snapping together. "Look, I flirted pretty hard with both of them when they first came down here. It never went anywhere. Least of all to the tent-cabin."

Ben reached for her and put his hands on her shoulders, rubbing at the tension he felt there. "I didn't think you slept with my brothers. I'm pretty sure they would have told me."

"Or Claire or Harmony would have. Do you think either one of them would be my friends if I'd been with their guys? Besides, once they fell, it was clear I had no chance with either one of them."

"Did you want a chance?" he had to know.

She appeared to consider his question for a few seconds. "Honestly? I think I wanted what they represent. They're hot. And real. And..." She shrugged beneath his gentle hold on her.

"Forever," he finished for her.

"No." She shook her head. "Not forever. I never wanted forever."

He stared at her, seeing a glimpse of something else in her eyes. Regret? Maybe. Not for what she'd missed out with Rick and Jake, though. Maybe she wished she hadn't insisted they keep this thing between the two of them "friendly."

"What do you want now?" he asked.

She licked her lips, her eyes wide. Before she could give him an answer, the buzzer on the oven went off and she literally slipped through his fingers. She stuck a toothpick into each of the layers, but he couldn't guess what she was checking. She was smiling, though. She must have seen what she was looking for.

"Done!" she said.

She grabbed the thick mitts set near the oven and took out the pans to set them on the cooling racks. At least he knew what those were now.

"All set?" he asked.

"No. Just a few more minutes, though. Then we take them out of the pans."

"We?"

"All right. I take them out of the pans."

"A few more minutes," he said.

She crossed her arms again. "Don't get any ideas. I don't want to talk about your brothers again, either."

"Nothing to talk about there."

She lifted her chin. "What about you? I'm sure you had a lot of fun out there in California."

"I did all right."

Her eyes ran over him, assessing and apparently liking what she saw. "You did all kinds of all right, didn't you?"

"Maybe. Does it matter?"

"Not at all." Her expression said otherwise, though. Her gaze slid away to the cooling pans. "Did you ever fall in love?"

"Nope," he answered easily.

Her face turned to him. "Never?"

He shook his head. "If I ever fall in love, I won't let go."

Her lips parted and he wished he could take the words back. Since when did he ever think about falling in love? It had to be the smell of chocolate cake. He must be getting a contact high.

She turned her back to him, facing the cake pans once more. "These are almost ready to take out of the pans."

"Tammy."

"Don't, Ben."

"Don't what?"

"We're not going there."

Her head dropped to her chest and he wanted to grab her and kiss away all this tension he'd caused. First with his questions about his brothers and now that crack about love? He was an idiot.

"Just forget what I said, honey." He wrapped his arms around her waist and gently pulled her against him. "I must be woozy from all the chocolate fumes."

She seemed to relax as she turned in his arms. "No more love talk. Got it?"

He nodded.

"And no more thinking I did any of those things I did with you with either of your brothers."

"Scout's honor."

A smile lifted one corner of her delectable mouth. "Why do I have trouble believing you were ever a boy scout?"

"Hey. Take me up on my offer and I promise I'll be prepared."

His statement was just what was needed at the moment. Light humor with a dose of heat. It seemed to put them both on more familiar footing.

She leaned up to kiss him, and then pushed him back. "Cakes."

He stepped away, turned on from their brief contact. She washed her hands and then made quick, careful work of the cakes. They were puffed and moist-looking and sitting proudly on Claire's cooling racks.

"Perfect." She wiped her hands on a dish towel and turned to him. "All set."

He stared at her for a long minute. She was pretty damn near perfect for him right now. She didn't want a commitment and neither did he. He should just keep the questions to a minimum and take whatever she gave him. It had always been enough with any other woman he'd known.

Why did it feel like it would never be enough with her?

***

Tammy returned from a tour that afternoon and handed her people off to Ollie. He was always the best at the in-house spiels and was currently lording over six other prospects in the gallery. He stood near the model of the development, and as she left him he gave her a pointed look. She just rolled her eyes. So he'd seen her leave with Ben bright and early this morning. Did he think they were at it like rabbits out in the golf cart?

"Not that it hadn't happened before," she murmured as she entered the breakroom.

"What's that, Tammy?" Rick asked.

She smiled at her boss. "Nothing. Looking forward to tonight's bash?"

"Should be fun," he said.

"And I'm sure the girls and I will get up to some mischief."

"You're headed up to Orlando."

"Yep. Lim-o-zine, my friend."

He smiled. "Harmony's excited about that, too."

"Excited about what?" Ben walked in and took her breath.

She didn't know what he'd been up to but his sleeves were rolled back and his tie was loosened just enough to show his strong throat.

"The limo for tonight," she rushed out.

A smile played around that mouth she was getting to know pretty well.

"Hey, it's nice to sit back and have somebody else drive once in a while," he said.

She gaped at him but, thankfully, Rick seemed to miss his meaning.

"Why don't you take off early, Tammy?" Rick asked.

"Thanks," she said. "I think I will."

Rick lifted his chin to Ben. "I'll see you later."

"Yep," Ben said.

Rick left and Tammy made a move to follow. Ben's hand on her arm stilled her. His touch made her pulse quicken and she couldn't afford this craziness at work.

"Ben," she said in warning.

He stroked her bare arm, and then dropped his hand. "I'm sorry about this morning."

"There's nothing to be sorry for," she told him. "Have fun tonight."

He nodded and she left him. Grabbing her bag from her office, she shut down her computer and locked up. Rapping on Claire's door, she found her friend in pretty much the same state. Her shoes were still off and standing precisely near her desk chair, like they always were when she was working.

"Come on, girl." Tammy stepped into the office. "We have some serious fun to get on tonight."

Claire grinned at her and slipped on her shoes. "Yeah, we do."

The two of them left the Sales Center. Claire dropped

184

Tammy off so she could get dressed before heading home to do the same.

"The limo is picking us up at seven," Claire told her.

Tammy saluted her. "Aye-aye, captain."

Claire laughed. "Thanks again for taking care of the cakes."

"No problem."

Claire fiddled with the gearshift, and then let out a breath. "So what's going on with you and Ben?"

Tammy continued to stare out the windshield, holding her expression. "Nothing's going on."

"You can't fool me with your salesgirl voice."

Tammy cursed softly. "Yeah, I know. But seriously, I won't let anything else happen with Ben."

"Anything *else*. Hmm. So you're still, how did you put it? Playing?"

"We're friends."

"With benefits."

Tammy shook her head. "Not exactly."

Claire snorted. "I wonder how long he'll play along."

Tammy didn't have an answer and she almost didn't want to know. "So what are you wearing tonight?"

"Okay, the subject is officially changed."

Tammy smiled and leaned back. Let any one of the ladies try to get her to talk about Ben tonight. She would be as silent as the grave. Or something like that.

Before long the four of them were happily settled in the back of a stretch Lincoln Navigator and on their way to Orlando, sipping the requisite champagne from crystal flutes. Tammy wore a short sheath dress in purple, topped by a lacy little cardigan a shade lighter. Claire wore a similar dress, done in what was now her signature poppy-orange color. As for the bride-to-be? Cassie was dressed like she was on the runway in Milan, and looking very young in her deceptively-blousy top over a short skirt.

"Cassie, you look hot," Tammy said. "And like you're not even old enough to drink."

Cassie laughed and tossed her thick, dark hair over one shoulder. "Thanks." Then she got a dreamy look in her eyes, eyes that were a lot like Ben's. "I can't believe I'm marrying Ty tomorrow."

"He's a lucky guy," Harmony said. She looked very nice tonight as well, with a washed silk dress in blues and greens. "He's getting a Chapman."

Claire looked pointedly at Tammy, who managed to keep

from giving anything away, and then turned back to Cassie. "I have to decorate your cake when I get home tonight, so don't let me drink too much."

Tammy laughed. "I say we let you get drunk enough to ask the waiter for a lap dance."

Claire blushed but she grinned. "Jake promised me one if I give him one after the bachelor party."

"Are they watching stag films?" Tammy asked, wiggling her eyebrows.

"Stag films?" Cassie blinked. "What are those?"

"Skin flicks, dear little sister," Harmony said. "I don't think they call them that anymore, though."

Tammy shrugged. "I thought it was fitting, seeing as they're going to be out in the woods."

Cassie laughed. "Too funny. Well, I say let them watch anything they like." She winked. "Get them all revved up."

Tammy grew quiet as the limo rolled on toward Orlando. Yeah, just let Ben get all revved up. She'd probably get a bootie call at two o'clock in the morning. Or maybe he'd stop by her townhouse on the way back from the far lakeshore.

He'd be all intense and hot. He would tell her how much he needed her. Tempt her to throw her vows, and any hope of self-preservation, to the winds.

"More liquid courage, please," she said, holding out her glass for another refill.

"Courage?" Harmony poured the champagne. "For what?"

"To keep a promise to myself."

The other three women exchanged looks ranging from confused to convinced. She would put on her big girl panties and keep them on, thanks.

No matter how much Ben tempted her to let them drop to the floor.

Chapter 14

"How about another hand?" Jake said, shuffling the deck.

The rest of them all voiced their agreement, clinking their beer bottles together over the felt-covered table. Ben figured they were all feeling no pain but no one was at the messy "this guy…this guy here…" stage. Cards and cigars, and more than a few dirty jokes, were about the extent of their wild night.

The tent-cabin was a pretty cool place. It was built of canvas and exposed wood-framed walls, and it had small windows set way up in each of the gable ends of the structure for ventilation. A sink, a two-burner stove and a small fridge made up the kitchen and there was a small table/desk combo set in one corner.

There were a few feminine touches, too. Hair and makeup brushes, creams and other stuff all but covered the small shelf set under the mirror nailed to one wall stud. The rag rug on the floor was faded but added a softness. He could see his sister liking it out here, especially since her guy spent most nights out here, too.

Jake had brought in the card table and chairs they used tonight, and it was a pretty tight fit. A big iron bed took up most of the space. Tammy had called it a love shack, and he guessed it would serve pretty well as one. He just didn't want to think about his little sister as half of the pair making use of that bed, thanks. He might have only known about her since May, but once he'd met her he found himself sharing his brothers' protectiveness.

The tent-cabin was situated at the edge of a pristine lake. The lakeshore was wilder than the one to the west or at the Cypress Inn, with thick trees and reeds bordering it instead of sandy beach. There was a trailer set to one side, filled with chairs and other stuff for the wedding set-up in the morning. He thought about the Spanish moss-draped trees and the lapping of the water and reasoned it was a pretty nice place to get married.

Ben drank his beer as his brother dealt the cards. There wasn't much teasing of the groom about wedding nights and breaking in the new wife tonight. That was really no surprise. The new wife in question was the little sister of all three of the other guys at the table. Still, he was having a good time hanging with his brothers and future brother-in-law.

"So this is pretty tame, huh bro?" Jake asked him, winking at Ty as he finished dealing and held his own hand of cards.

"It's nice," Ben said. "I've been to a few bachelor parties I can't even remember."

"I took Jake out to the strip club in Melbourne for his," Rick said as he looked at his own cards before tossing a few chips into the center to ante up. "Out on the east coast."

Jake laughed and shook his head. "And what happens in Melbourne, stays in Melbourne."

Ben arched a brow, but Jake just added his own chips to open. "Kidding, bro. The view was pretty good, though."

"The last stag I went to was back in Santa Cruz." Ben looked at his lousy hand of cards and held up two fingers. He took the two cards Jake dealt him and set his hand face down on the table. "For a friend of a friend. Involved more liquor and women I think were at least as pretty as the three of you."

"Got a few lap dances, did you?" Ty asked.

Ben dipped his head. "I think I ended up with my pants around my ankles a few times, but yeah."

Jake whistled. "Sounds like a party I went to out in Aspen a couple of years ago."

Ben grinned and lifted his bottle to salute him. He'd known Jake was a player before settling down with Claire. It didn't seem like the guy missed any of that life, though.

"How about you, Ty?" Rick asked, taking one card and keeping his poker face. Ben already knew that the guy rarely gave anything away. "Any naked skeletons in your closet?"

Ty gave his trademark "aw-shucks" expression and shrugged. "Not too many, no."

"Hmm," Jake teased. "Sounds like there's a story there."

Ty shrugged. "Maybe. But if you think I'm going to tell it to my bride's three brothers, you're crazy."

"Fair enough," Ben said.

Play continued around the table until both Ben and Ty folded and it was down to Jake and Rick. Jake wore his every expression on his face, much like their sister. It was clear he had a killer hand and it was just as clear that you couldn't tell what Rick was holding.

"I raise you five dollars," Rick said, his gaze even.

Ben looked from him to Jake, seeing the sparkle in his brother's eyes. Apparently Ty was enjoying this particular game as well, for a crooked smile brought out one of his dimples.

"I see your five and raise you ten," Jake said, leaning toward Rick.

Rick eyed him, and then added more of his own chips to the pile. "I call."

Jake spread his cards, showing a royal flush. Hearts, of all things. Fitting, given tomorrow's event. "I've got you, bro."

Rick turned over his hand, showing an impressive full house of queens over jacks, but it didn't beat Jake's.

"I should have known better," Rick said to Ben as Jake took the markers. "The guy has no poker face. I should have known he had a killer hand."

"Yeah," Jake put in. "If it had come down to you and Ben, it would've been different. He's got your deadpan down for sure. Pure mystery."

"Me?" Ben was surprised. "I didn't know I had a look of mystery."

"Don't sound all romantic about it," Jake laughed. "I just mean that you're a little bit like our big bro here. Still waters, and all that."

"That's what Cassie says about me," Ty said.

"And let that be the last thing you tell us Cassie says about you." Rick said.

Ty chuckled. "No argument here."

Jake got up and grabbed a few more beers out of the little fridge. "Another one, Ben?"

Ben shook his head. "I don't think so. I'm driving."

"You're welcome to crash out here with me," Ty said. "These two need to go home so they can be all pretty for the wedding tomorrow."

"And what about you?" Jake asked Ty.

"My tux is hanging over there," Ty answered, indicating a garment bag hung from a hook on one of the framing studs. "My mother is taking care of Riley in the morning. I just have to shower, shave and I'm ready.

"Ben has it even easier," Rick said. "He just has to show up with the other guests."

"I don't know how easy tomorrow morning will be," Ben said. "You know Bill is staying at the inn."

Rick's lips thinned a little. "Cassie told me."

"At least you'll only have to share the breakfast part of the B and B with him," Jake said. "Speaking of which, what's up with you and Tammy?"

Ben leveled a look at him, hoping he really did have his oldest brother's deadpan. "Nothing's up."

"Bullshit," Rick said.

Ben gaped at him. "Why do you say that?"

"I work with her," Rick went on. "And I've seen you around her. Your tongue was practically hanging out this afternoon."

"She's hot." Ben fiddled with his discarded cards. "I'm a guy. It was just a natural reaction."

194

"I'm not accusing you of anything," Rick said. "I'm just making an observation."

"All right, then," Ben said.

Jake folded his arms and leaned back. Ben could read the speculation on his face, as clear as his winning hand had been.

"What?" Ben asked him.

Jake just shrugged. "Seems to me we had this little talk already."

Ben stood, so not ready to have this conversation again any time soon. "And that's my cue. Guys, I'll see you tomorrow." His brothers nodded and Ben shook Ty's hand, clapping him on the shoulder. "Good luck tomorrow, man. You're getting a great girl."

Ty smiled broadly now. "Don't I know it."

Ben left them and got back in his Jeep. He'd had a good time with these guys. Comfortable. That last bit shocked the hell out of him. He'd only known them for a few months but they'd treated him the same way they did each other. He'd gotten a lot more than a change of scenery when he'd come down here.

A welcoming family. *Check.* Dedication and enthusiasm for his newest project. *Check.* A hot woman to tempt him to try and win her over. *Check* and *check.*

195

He might not have come to Cypress Corners with the intentions to stay, but it sure looked like the place was doing its level best to convince him this was just where he wanted to be.

Roots grew fast and deep here, though. Just look at how fast his siblings had settled themselves. Fast and deep he could do, if he could finally manage to get Tammy into bed. But roots?

His life in California left him no real moorings. He'd relished a laid-back lifestyle and had no real connections now that his mother was gone.

How could he settle anywhere if he didn't know how?

***

Tammy stepped out of the limo in front of her townhouse, wobbling a little on her heels. Laughter from inside reached her as she waved goodnight and stumbled up the steps to her door. Whoa, she hadn't had this much to drink since…she couldn't remember exactly when right now, but it was a long friggin' time ago.

She managed to unlock her door and close it behind her with a slam. "Shh," she murmured, kicking off her shoes.

She made her way to the kitchen and grabbed a glass and filled it with water through the refrigerator door. A few gulps of the cold liquid and she felt steadier. Her pretty house was still spinning just a little bit, though. Man, her couch looked comfy. Flopping down on it, she shifted and put her feet up on the very nice, distressed wood coffee table.

She'd had a great time tonight. Her friends were so nice. Even Cassie, whom she'd only known since the spring, was as warm to her as she was to Claire and Harmony.

True, Tammy had flirted with all of their guys in her time. She'd been honest with Ben about that. It pissed her off when he'd hinted that she'd been with his brothers, though. Really! Sure she would have tumbled into bed with either one of them if they'd asked back then. Heck, she would have given Ty a chance to tame her if he'd wanted to. But that was before they fell in love with their women. And now she only appreciated them in the abstract for the hot guys they were. Now Ben, on the other hand.

Him, she could have. Any way she wanted for as long as she wanted. Or as short. Why didn't she just give in and sleep with him? It would be good. So good. He had moves she could appreciate. He'd liked what she'd done to him a couple of times, too. He scared her, though. He meant things she knew she wasn't ready for, no matter how much he denied it.

Upending her little party purse, she found her phone and

scrolled through the contacts. He was in there. He'd put his phone number in there before she'd left his room at the inn.

"He thought I didn't notice." She smiled to herself. "Silly boy."

She tapped the text symbol and started typing. She would tell him just what she thought about his insinuations…that word took a long time to type…about her and his brothers. *Send.* About how she wasn't going to give in no matter what. *Send.* She would tell him just what she would do to him if she did give in. *Send.* And how pretty his eyes were. *Send.* And how much fun she had with his very nice body. *Send.*

"There!" She let the phone slip from her fingers and leaned her head back. "Take that, Mr. Ben Chapman."

She took a deep breath before standing once more. Stripping off her dress, she made her way up the stairs to her bedroom and stretched out on the bed in her underwear.

Sometime later, she cracked open an eye to see the morning sun peeking through her blinds. Her mouth was dry and her face felt sticky. No big surprise there. She'd fallen asleep in half of her clothes and all of her makeup. No hangover headache today, though. She'd count herself lucky there.

Glancing at the clock on her nightstand, she saw it was

almost nine o'clock. Stretching until she groaned, she tried to focus on the coming day. Thank God she had no duties regarding the Chapman/Walsh nuptials. She had all day to rest up for the ceremony this afternoon and the party to follow.

After washing her face and spending a long time under the shower, she felt more like herself. As she waited for her coffee maker to give up the goods, she picked up her discarded shoes and clothes from the floor. Her purse had spilled all over the couch, so she gathered up the lip gloss, card wallet, keys and phone from the cushions. Something niggled at the back of her mind as she plugged the phone into its charger. Something about Ben.

God, had she drunk-dialed Ben last night? No. Had she raised any sort of flag in his direction he would have been over in a flash. They would have ended up in her bed, too. Her conviction was never very strong around him as it was. If he'd made his move last night, she knew she would have been all over him. This morning she'd woken up alone, so she took that as a sign of some strength, anyway. Oh, but he would have looked very nice tangled up in her Egyptian cotton sheets this morning.

She dressed to grab some relaxation before she had to get

ready for the wedding. And like that Sunday morning she'd run into Ben, she headed for the lakeshore reserved for guests of the Cypress Inn.

As she'd hoped, the small beach was deserted. She spread her towel on one of the loungers and dropped her crocheted cover up. Letting out a breath, she stretched out and closed her eyes.

A throat-clearing caught her attention about an hour later, and she peeped one eye open to see a big guy standing beside her lounger. For a second she thought it was Ben. The guy was certainly built like him. Shading her eyes with her hand, she soon saw it wasn't him. It was pretty close, though.

"Hello, Mr. Chapman," she said.

"Hello, Tammy." Bill Chapman smiled down at her. "I see the view here at the inn has gotten better."

He was joking with her, or trying to charm her or something. She'd been acquainted with Bill for years now, and knew his M.O. He never gave compliments without cause, she knew she looked good, and he never expended any effort on anything that wouldn't benefit his bottom line. Something was bugging him today.

Sitting up, she turned so her feet rested on the cool sand.

"Are you enjoying your stay?"

He nodded, sitting on the lounger next to hers like Ben had. "The place is nice." His use of flattery didn't extend to the inn, apparently. "Have you had a chance to get with Ben?"

She was glad she still wore her sunglasses after getting hit with that question. Although, knowing Bill, she guessed he was referring to the new development.

"I have. He's excited about the plans he's creating."

Bill nodded. "He's good."

Tammy figured that was high praise coming from him.

"I bet you're looking forward to the wedding," she offered.

His expression changed then, His brows drew together and lines formed to bracket his mouth. She'd never seen him as anything but capable and commanding Bill Chapman, and the difference was telling.

"Yes." His answer was curt but a little on the warm side. "Cassandra will be a beautiful bride."

Tammy simply nodded. The girl was as gorgeous as her brothers and would be stunning in the dress she'd chosen. Tammy had seen it. Lots of lace and pearls but very simple.

He came to his feet again. "I should head back. You going to the wedding?"

"I wouldn't miss it," she said.

He nodded again, running one hand over his hair like Ben sometimes did. She wondered if Ben knew he shared more than DNA with Bill.

"Then I'll see you there."

Tammy watched Ben's father make his way back up to the inn. She knew he was estranged from his kids. Rick had next to nothing to do with him and Jake barely tolerated him when he visited. Cassie was the apple of her father's eye, but even she had little to do with him since he'd told them about Ben.

As for Ben? She didn't see any affection coming from him in Bill's direction. It was so different from her and her family. Yes, they could be overwhelming at times. But she loved them and they loved her. That was never in question.

At around three o'clock, she got in her car to drive over to the wedding venue. She was wearing one of her favorite sheath dresses, this one of creamy lace that was perfect for a fall wedding in Florida. She held her hair back with a wide headband, and flirty peep-toe pumps finished her outfit.

As she drove, she felt a tingle of anticipation. She'd see Ben today. God, how good would he look all cleaned up? Once again, that niggle of memory teased her. That impression that she'd had some sort of contact with Ben while she'd been more than a little bit tipsy.

She pulled up to the line of cars bracketing the open-air chapel. The lakeshore looked enchanting and very romantic, all dressed up for Ty and Cassie's wedding. White and yellow bunting and flowers in the same colors draped low branches on the towering Cypress trees and hugged the poles holding up a canopy of thick, white ribbons overhead. Rows of white folding chairs, separated down the middle, created seating and an aisle. It was a gorgeous setting for a ceremony that was happily anticipated by friends and family alike.

Leaving her car to one of the valets hired for the event, she turned to walk beneath the canopy and ran right into the man in question. Yes, Ben looked good. His dark gray suit, crisp white shirt and blue tie did him justice. The stubble was gone from his cheeks and his dimple was in full view. And why was that? Because he was grinning at her, that was why.

"What's up?" she asked, tilting her head to the side.

In answer, he simply held up his phone.

And just like that, she remembered. The texts she'd sent him last night. *Oh, God.*

Jeez, she was in for it now.

Chapter 15

Ben had watched Tammy approach from the second she'd stepped out of her sweet little convertible and left the valet kid staring after her ass. After riding to the far lakeshore with Jake, he'd left his brothers to their wedding duties and had nothing to do but wait for her to arrive. There was the little matter of her dirty sexting last night that simply had to be addressed. He couldn't wait to hear her excuses.

Her dress was a shade lighter than her skin and hugged every delectable curve of her body. The lacy hem fell just past mid-thigh, and swished as she walked confidently on heels over the sandy ground. A whole lot of leg showed in that dress. Long, silky, smoothly-muscled legs he'd had wrapped around his neck just a few days ago. *Damn.*

Her cheeks were red as she glanced at his phone. He watched as her expression swiftly turned cool. "That's your phone."

He nodded. "Mmm-hmm."

"And?"

"I received some pretty hot texts last night. From your number." He scrolled through the texts that were waiting for him

204

this morning. "It's a real shame you sent these after I was already all tucked into my lonely bed."

"Shh." She flicked her eyes around and leaned closer. "No bed talk."

"Okay." He used his thumb to pull up one particular message. "Now, this one here I really like."

"Ben," she whispered in obvious warning.

"Yeah, this one. The one where you say just what you want to do to—"

"Stop." Her eyes narrowed. "I didn't remember sending those texts."

"No?"

She flicked some of her shining hair over one creamy shoulder and shook her head. "Not until you waved your phone in my face."

He tucked his phone back in his pocket. "So what am I supposed to do with this information?"

"What information?"

"Ah, Tammy." He leaned closer to speak into her ear, taking in a breath of her sweet, floral scent. "All of those naughty things you want to do to my fine self."

Her cool demeanor shifted and the speculation in her hazel

eyes nearly brought him to his knees. Yeah, he wanted to make good on every suggestion she'd sent him. And, right at this moment, she looked like she wanted him to.

"Well?" he prompted.

The string quartet seated near the front of the open-air chapel began to play softly, saving her from making an answer. They both turned their attention to the front of the chapel. An arbor was erected there, and Ty and best-man Jake stood waiting.

"Looks like we should take our seats," he said. Holding out his arm, he smiled at her. "Miss?"

"Oh, you just had to pour on the charm, too?" she grumbled as she placed her hand in the crook of his elbow.

"Seems to me I need all the help I can get."

Her lips curved a little bit and he took that as a point in his favor. "Where to?"

Most of the seats were filled, with the exception of the ones in the rows closest to the front. Unofficially reserved for family, he guessed. He paused at the third row of chairs on the right that had a couple seats free on the aisle. "Here?"

She nodded and he claimed the second seat in. "I thought I'd leave you the aisle," he said.

She smiled more fully now. "Thanks."

As they settled into their seats, he turned and noticed his father walking down the aisle toward them. Ben gave him a nod and Bill sat down directly behind him.

"Ben. Tammy," he said.

"Hello again, Mr. Chapman," Tammy said.

"Again?" Ben asked.

"Tammy and I met on the beach by the inn this morning," Bill said.

"Yes," Tammy said, turning to Ben once more. "I was dressed much more casually."

"But you looked just as pretty," Bill added.

Ben puzzled over that for a second before it struck him. The beach at the inn. Bill had seen Tammy in her bikini. Ben didn't think Bill was shopping for wife number five, but you never knew with the guy. In fact, sometimes the only contact he and his mother would have with him over the years was a wedding announcement.

A knot formed in his belly. Christ, was he jealous of his father? He looked at Tammy and saw she was staring at him again, laughter in her eyes. Apparently she guessed where his mind went and found it funny. He would take that as a good sign. He really couldn't see her sexting his father in the middle of the night.

The quartet began to play more loudly and the guests turned in their seats to watch the procession. Ty's little niece, Riley, was the first to walk down the aisle. She wore a puffy dress in pink and sparkly shoes that had to be his sister Cassie's doing. She was an adorable little thing, with light blond hair and big blue eyes. Holding a wicker basket of white rose petals, she dumped handfuls as she walked solemnly to the front of the open-air chapel.

"My God, she's adorable," Tammy said softly.

Ben silently agreed. His nephew Nick wasn't one to be outdone by the flower girl, and hurried to walk close behind her with the pillow holding the rings. His suit was a miniature of Jake and Ty's black, and he beamed a smile at everyone as he passed their row. When he came up to Bill, he furrowed his brow. Bill waved at him and Nick lifted his hand a little in response. Then Nick caught sight of him and Tammy.

A smile split his face and he waved wildly. "Hi, Uncle Ben! Hi, Tammy!" His voice was pitched in a little boy's idea of a stage-whisper, and from the soft laughter around them it was clear everyone had heard him.

"Hey, buddy," Ben whispered. "Good job."

Nick clutched the pillow tighter to his chest. "Yep."

Ben chuckled as a warmth spread through him. Tammy touched his hand and he glanced over at her.

"He likes you," she said softly.

Ben grinned. "Yep," he said, mimicking Nick.

Claire came down the aisle next, followed by Harmony. They looked really pretty in dresses a darker pink than little Riley's. Then a swell of music came from the quartet and everyone stood.

He heard Tammy gasp and Ben followed her gaze to see his little sister framed by the bunting stretched over the entry. She was on Rick's arm, and Ben felt a shift in his chest. These people were his family. He caught Cassie's eye and she beamed a smile at him as she and Rick came closer. Turned toward the back as he was, Ben could see Bill's face. The guy looked stunned, and his eyes were misty.

"Cassandra," he said on a breath.

Ben exchanged a look with Tammy, who raised her brows. It was clear Bill loved their little sister. When Cassie reached Bill, she leaned over and gave him a kiss on the cheek. Tammy sniffled and Ben felt his throat go tight. What was it about weddings, anyway?

Rick nodded at their father and continued to lead Cassie to the arbor where Ty and Jake stood waiting. Ben got over his emotional storm, small though it was, and sat with the rest of the guests. He didn't know why but he took Tammy's hand in his. She held on to him and it made him feel more grounded.

He didn't know what they were right now. They weren't even fuck-buddies. But holding her hand made it easier to get through this ceremony involving so many of his new family. He sure as hell wasn't going to cry. No friggin' way.

After vows were exchanged and the happy couple was announced to the gathering, the bridal party went off for pictures. He escorted Tammy to the valet line for the drive to the Clubhouse for drinks and dinner.

"That was amazing," she said, clutching her fingers like she wanted to hold his hand again.

He wouldn't say no if she did. That was for sure.

"They look so damn happy." He smiled. "At the risk of handing in my Man Card, I'll admit I nearly teared up in there."

She smiled brightly. "I definitely did." She handed her ticket to one of the valets and turned to him. "Did you bring the Jeep?"

"No. I hitched a ride with Jake. I was kind of hoping you

would give me a ride to the Clubhouse."

She smirked. "Letting me drive again, are you?"

A spark of heat stroked over him. "Tamara."

She lost her smile, her eyes big. Before they could trade anymore innuendo, her car was brought around and they climbed in.

He would have her tonight. In his bed or hers, it didn't matter. He had to, or he would go crazy. No question. He had to be really careful, though. Weddings tended to make women think about forever. Yeah, he'd bagged a few bridesmaids in his time but he made sure they knew what it was all about.

Tonight could go either way, given the woman in question. Tammy could jump him and forget all about her worries of commitment and forever. Or she could shy away from anything else with him, thinking to keep herself safe from what she thought she saw in him. He didn't care at the moment.

He guessed she didn't know what she really wanted, except for him. He sure as hell didn't know what he wanted himself, except for her under him. And over him.

Tonight, they would make each other happy and leave the rest of it alone.

***

Tammy stood on the edge of the dancefloor in the Clubhouse's large event hall, taking small sips of champagne from the flute in her hand. The dinner had been delicious, crab cakes and big steaks done perfectly accompanied by adorable little baby vegetables and potatoes. The toasts and the couple's first dance was all that it should be.

She stood here now, all choked up. At a wedding! Jeez, she hadn't even cried at her little sister's wedding last May. There was just something about seeing two people so perfect for each other in a setting so perfect for the two of them that did it to her. Seeing Ben choke up had been eye-opening, too. The guy was growing attached to his family in spite of himself.

Ty swayed with his new bride on the dancefloor again, sharing the kind of smiles Tammy had never seen flashed in her own direction. When Ty's niece joined them, her arms wrapped around Cassie's waist, Tammy almost lost it.

"They make a gorgeous couple, don't they?" Lettie asked.

Tammy turned to smile at Lettie. She was dressed like a grand lady tonight, with ropes of pearls and a dress that might look silly on a woman her age if Lettie looked like a woman her age. She even had on kitten heels instead of her ever-present crocs.

"They really do." Tammy glanced at the table where Ty's mother sat with a big smile on her face. "How's Ty's mom feeling today?"

"Oh, Sharon isn't going to let a little something like Fibromyalgia dim her bulb at her son's wedding."

"She does look pretty happy."

"Why not? Her son is getting the perfect woman for him."

"Cassie is that." Tammy watched the couple share a kiss, and raised her flute when those around her began to applaud. "I think they're pretty perfect for each other."

"Yes. And seeing a handsome man dressed to the nines is sure a nice way to spend an evening."

Like a reflex, her eyes strayed to where Ben stood talking to Jake and Claire. Yeah, Jake looked great but it was Ben who took her breath away. Maybe it was because she'd seen him with a lot fewer clothes on. She recalled how sculpted that body was. The broad, hard chest. The flat, ridged belly. Those strong legs and arms that tangled so nicely with hers.

"Now there's a look I haven't seen on your gorgeous face before," Lettie said.

Tammy blinked and faced her again. "What's that?"

"Pure desire, honey." She leaned closer, dropping her voice.

"You want that man in the worst way."

"Oh, Lettie," Tammy said in a whisper. "I want that man in the *best* way."

Lettie stared for a second, and then let loose with a brash yet musical laugh. "I'm proud of you, girl."

Tammy grinned at her. "Well, Claire assures me I'm following in your footsteps."

"Is that so?" Lettie sipped her own champagne and slowly nodded. "Then you best get busy. By your age I'd already won my Mr. Fairfax." She winked. "In the best way."

"I'm not trying to win anybody," Tammy said.

"If you say so. But if the look he just threw in your direction was any hungrier your panties would melt right off."

"Lettie!" Tammy chuckled. "You're just this side of too much, aren't you?"

Lettie gave a very elegant shrug of one shoulder. "I suppose I have to be, don't I?"

"I wouldn't have you any other way," Tammy told her.

"Hmm. Seems to me that line lacks the punch it would have if this beautiful man had said it."

Tammy was about to ask her which beautiful man she was referring to when she felt Ben standing just behind her. His scent hit her first, and then his warmth surrounded her.

"Lettie, you are a vision tonight," he drawled.

Lettie's blue eyes danced. "My dear Ben Chapman. I told you that accent is wasted on me. Now Tammy here? I just bet she'd faint dead away if you turned the full effect of those eyes and that dimple on her."

Tammy closed her eyes and prayed for strength as she turned to welcome Ben into her and Lettie's tight little circle. "Hey, Ben."

"Hey, Tammy."

His eyes and his dimple did all the magic Lettie just predicted. Melting panties, all right. Lettie's soft chuckle told her that the woman didn't miss the heat between them.

"Oh, just look," Lettie said. "Sharon is crying now." She touched Ben's arm and gave it a squeeze neither he nor Tammy missed. "Ty's poor mother has been rain and sunshine all day. I'll say farewell to you two now."

"See you, Lettie," Tammy said.

"Good bye, Lettie," Ben put in.

Lettie gave him another squeeze, raising her graceful brows, and left them.

Ben's cheeks were a little bit red. "Why do I just feel like

215

that was a test?"

Tammy laughed. "Don't worry. I'm pretty sure you passed."

He smiled, that deadly dimple winking into sight again. "So, you kept to yourself tonight."

"Did I?" She thought for a second. "Seems to me I mingled just the right amount."

"Is there a right amount? I wouldn't know." His brow furrowed a bit. "I just hung around with Jake and Claire most of the night."

"You're closest to him." Tammy shrugged. "It makes sense you'd be more comfortable around him."

"Closest." He looked genuinely confused. "I guess so. I do feel a little less out of place with Jake."

She stared at him. He really didn't think he fit with these people? "They're your family, Ben."

"Yeah." His expression grew shuttered. "I know."

She stroked his arm as Lettie had, resisting the urge to give him a squeeze. "It'll get easier."

"What will get easier?"

"Family."

He smirked at her, his eyes twinkling now. "Has yours gotten any easier?"

She waved a hand. "That's a whole different deal. I've known them for twenty-seven years. It's about as easy as it's ever going to get."

"Hmm." One strong hand stroked his jaw. "Interesting."

Did she even want to know? Yes. Yes, she did.

"What's interesting?" she asked.

"You just told me something about yourself."

She flushed a little. "I've never kept anything a secret."

"Ah, I think you have."

"Yeah?"

Nodding, he stepped closer. "You're keeping a very important secret, Tamara."

She shivered as she stared into his eyes. "What's the secret?" she breathed.

"Just how much you want me."

Her whole body grew hot and her knees wobbled a little.

"That's no secret, Ben."

His eyes grew dark. "Then let's get out of here."

It would be so easy to give in to what was clearly between them. To give him what they both wanted. Then why should she fight it? It wasn't like his family was paying attention to them at the moment. And she wanted him so much she could hardly breathe. The few encounters they'd shared were clearly leading up to something pretty fantastic.

"Okay." She drained her champagne flute and set it down on the nearest table. "We'll just see if you can keep all the promises in those pretty eyes of yours."

"Honey, you can count on it."

And just like that, any hope she had of staying in the friend zone melted along with her panties.

Chapter 16

Ben was glad Tammy was driving, because he was so hard he could barely sit in his seat. She parked behind her townhouse and let them in through the garage. That was the extent of his notice, though. His attention was fixed on her and how quickly he could get her out of that pretty lace dress.

She stepped out of her heels and came really close to him. "I can't believe I'm breaking my own rule."

"Are you sure about this?" he asked.

If she wasn't, he could manage to get himself back to the inn. He'd walk all the way there, if it meant not taking advantage of the romance of a wedding.

She nodded and took his hand. "I'm sure."

He followed her up the stairs to her bedroom at the back of the townhouse. The lights were dim but her silhouette was enough to drive him crazy. "Come here."

She did, that incredible body of hers barely touching him. He cupped her face, bringing his mouth to hers for a long kiss. Her lips parted in the next second, letting him taste her. Champagne and that sweetness that was all her. Grabbing her beneath her fine little ass, he lifted her tight against him. She held on to his shoulders, and all but wrapped herself around him.

"God, Tammy." He slipped his hands under the lacy hem of her dress and palmed her ass with both hands. "You feel so damn good."

"I am damn good." She moved to nip him on the side of his neck and he groaned. "But we have to make one thing clear, Ben."

He froze, and then let out a breath. "Please don't tell me you're not going to sleep with me."

She laughed, a throaty sound that stroked over him. "Oh, I won't say that tonight."

He set her down on her feet but kept his hands tight on her. "Then, what?"

"Just because we're stepping out of the friend zone doesn't mean this is anything more than what it looks like."

He looked over her, from her pretty bare feet, up those sinful legs and over the cleavage begging for his lips. When he reached her face, he saw her eyes were dark and her lips parted.

"It looks damn good to me, Tamara."

She put her hands on the sides of his head and pulled him in close. "Let's keep this light and easy, Ben. And no one gets hurt."

Her words cut through his horny haze a little. "I'd never hurt you."

She smiled and turned in his arms, holding all that silky hair up off her neck. "Unzip me."

His fingers fumbled for a second on the tiny zipper pull at the back of her dress, but he managed to do a decent job of revealing more of her delectable skin. "I've fantasized about unzipping that sexy sports bra you had on the other day." He dropped a kiss between her shoulder blades. "This is even better."

She shivered and turned as her dress pooled around her feet. "Not that you don't look good enough to eat, but let's get you out of these clothes."

He shrugged out of his jacket and loosened his tie as she began to work the buttons of his shirt free. "You know, I can think of a couple of things we could do with this tie."

She bit her plump bottom lip and shook her head. "Oh, you don't have to tie me down, Big Ben." She finished with the buttons of his shirt and pushed it off of his shoulders. "I'm not going anywhere."

He kicked off his shoes and dropped the rest of his clothes in a pile as he urged her toward her bed. He vaguely noticed that

221

her room was pretty. Not fussy but still feminine. Just like her.

She stretched out beneath him on smooth-as-silk sheets, running her hands over him. "I don't know what I want to do first."

"Everything, Tammy." He grabbed one of her hands and brought it to his lips. "Everything first."

She gave a throaty laugh and he licked and kissed his way down her neck to her breasts. Her lacy strapless bra was a memory and he cupped her flesh. Arching, she pressed upward into his palms and he wanted to touch every inch of her at once. She tasted so sweet as he nuzzled her, puckering tight against his tongue when he took a nipple into his mouth.

"Yes," she breathed, running her fingers through his hair.

He slid a hand between her thighs and dipped a finger into her. She was wet and ready. He nearly groaned. Her fingers were quick as they reached down between them and grabbed onto his cock. Her touch was perfect, and he thought he'd come in her hand if he didn't get himself in control and quick.

"Wait a sec." He took her hand and gently lifted it off of him. "Condom."

She nodded, coming up on her elbows to watch as he fished in a pocket of his suit pants to find a packet.

"Armed and ready?" she teased.

"Hey, I told you I'd be prepared."

She nodded, her eyes hot on him as he sheathed himself. "That you did."

Seeing her leaning back like that, her body flushed and ready and his for tonight, made him stop and stared for a long minute. Then he covered her body again, feeling every inch of her respond as she began to purr. Reaching down to lift and bend one of her legs, he spread her wide open and sank into her.

She clenched him deep inside, closing her eyes as she began to move against him. He braced himself on his hands, staring down at her as she took him again and again. Damn, he'd fantasized about this. But the reality? It beat his fantasies to hell and back.

She took everything he gave her. Fast and hard. Slow and easy. He rode her and almost came out of himself as his pleasure built.

"Ben." She panted in his ear, her arms wrapped around his neck. "God, Ben."

He thought he answered, but he wasn't even sure when he'd buried his face in her neck. He breathed her in, sweet and hot, as he moved closer and closer to climax. She made it first, thank

God. As she crested, crying out in her pleasure, he continued to move and was rewarded when she came again. Only then did he finally give up, climaxing with a shout.

Sometime later, he wasn't sure how much time had passed, he held her close. He was still inside of her. Still stunned by the best sex he'd ever had. She nuzzled against his throat, her body still clenching him as he let out a moan.

"Tammy, honey." He sucked in a breath and eased off of her. "That was almost worth the wait."

She hummed as she turned to face him. "Almost, huh?"

He brushed a long strand of her hair off her face, staring into those sleepy hazel eyes. "It was amazing. Don't get me wrong. I thought I'd die from the waiting, though."

She laughed, the sound light as if she didn't have a worry in the world. Well, she shouldn't. She'd come twice around him.

"I wasn't being a tease, you know," she said.

He nodded. "Oh, I know."

She blinked at him. "You know why I fought this?"

"Yeah. I know. Do you?"

She stretched her naked body and he didn't hide the fact that he took in every inch of her.

There was a smile of pure pleasure on her flushed and

beautiful face. "At this moment, I have no idea."

He laughed softly and hugged her to him. "And we have all night."

"Have a few more of those condoms, do you?" she asked.

He nodded again.

Grinning, she pushed him onto his back, straddling his belly. "Then buckle up. I'm driving."

***

Tammy grabbed the two pumpkin spice lattes she'd bought and headed out into the autumn sunshine. Lettie was in her usual place in the courtyard, but today Tammy just nodded and kept walking. It didn't matter that Lettie waved at her like her smock was on fire. The woman would take one look at her and see every little thing Ben had done to her Saturday night. And probably guess every little thing Tammy had done right back to him.

Sunday they'd tangled a few more times before she finally kicked him out. Hanging around on a Sunday afternoon was way too cozy. And way too much of a couple-y thing to do. They weren't a couple. They were friends with benefits, and heck there were some fantastic benefits with this particular arrangement. It was only a matter of time before every Chapman in Cypress knew about this, though.

"Look at you," Ollie said as she walked into the Sales Center.

She held in a groan. *And here we go.* She stopped, making a show of looking over her pressed and usual outfit. "What?"

Ollie came closer. "You got some!" he rasped.

Her cheeks flamed but she held her chin high. "The wedding was just lovely, Ollie. Thanks for asking."

Ollie laughed, and then moved to take one of the cups she held.

"Nope," she said, pulling it out of his reach. "This is for Claire."

"Hmm. Chapmans get everything." Ollie winked. "And I mean everything."

"Stop it," she said without heat.

"I want the details, girl."

She bit her lip and leaned close to him. "He totally earns that nickname you gave him."

Ollie's eyes went round and he whistled. "Good for him. And for you."

Tammy just left him, headed for Claire's office. Her friend was staring at her computer, twirling a lock of hair.

226

"What's up?" Tammy asked.

Claire turned in her chair, her eyes zeroing in on the latte. "Numbers. Is that for me?"

"Who else?"

Tammy handed her the cup and waited while Claire took a sip and burned her lip, like she did just about every morning.

"Ouch." Claire touched her upper lip with one finger. "So worth it, though."

Tammy smiled and took a careful sip from her own cup. "Fall in a cup."

"So you and Ben disappeared Saturday night."

Tammy gave her an even look, and then leaned her hip on Claire's desk. "Before you even ask, yes. I broke my promise."

Claire's grin was bright. And very irritating.

"Why are you smiling?" Tammy asked.

"I just won ten bucks."

Tammy rolled her eyes. "What is with your family and betting on me?"

"It's a guy version of gossip. Which they insist they don't do, by the way."

"I guess telling you not to tell Jake is out of the question?"

"Mmm hmm." Claire nodded. "What's the big deal?"

227

Tammy thought about her question, taking another careful sip of pumpkin spice. "The big deal is, this isn't leading anywhere. The big deal is, this will be over before Ben breaks ground in the new development. The big deal is…I don't know what the big deal is really."

"Then you really don't care if everyone knows?"

Tammy stood again. "Don't go taking out an ad in the *Cypress Scoop* or anything."

"No? You don't have a barbeque grill to sell?"

Tammy smiled at her friend. "Thanks, Claire. You're one of the good ones."

Claire's expression was suddenly serious. "I have your back, Tammy. You were there for me when I needed you and I'll gladly do the same."

Tammy's throat grew tight. Last year, before Claire and Jake got together for good, Tammy had taken Claire to the hospital and been there for her while waiting to hear whether or not Jake's latest death-defying stunt would do just that. It was the least Tammy could do, in her opinion. She knew it had been important to Claire, and that had taken them from work buddies to true friends.

"Thanks, but I'll be just fine," Tammy said. "I know this

isn't for keeps."

Claire blinked at her. "Do you want it to be? You know. For keeps?"

Tammy waited to be seized with the panic that usually came with such talk, but this morning she was just mildly irritated at the thought. It must be all those orgasms.

"I don't," she told Claire.

Claire didn't look convinced but she was soon drinking her latte again and that gave Tammy the pause she needed to get out of her office.

"Catch you later," Claire said, wrapping her hands lovingly around the cardboard cup.

Tammy left her and walked down to her office. Her sanctuary. She'd earned this. She'd been at Cypress for five years now. She started when she knew barely anything about property, escrow, listings, or specs. Mr. Forbes was a great teacher in the beginning, but when Rick came on as Sales Director she came into her own.

Settling into her chair, she took the lid off her coffee and clicked her laptop to bring up today's schedule. She didn't have any tours this morning, since Rick called for a meeting at ten to introduce the new builder. Ben would probably be there as well.

She let out a breath. She had to run into him fully clothed sometime soon, right? At least there would be a conference table between them. Although, knowing him, he'd sit right next to her. And probably play footsie.

She tingled more than a little bit at that. Clicking through her schedule, she sent it to her phone for reference and closed out.

A quick knock came at her door and she braced herself for more not-so-subtle innuendo from Ollie. Instead, Jessie poked her little blond head inside.

"Hey, Jessie."

"Did you hear?" Jessie looked a little panicked. "About today's meeting?"

"It's on our schedules, so yes." Tammy turned to face her. "What's the big deal?"

"He's going to be there."

"Yes, Jessie. They're all going to be there. Be more specific."

"The new builder guy." She covered her face with her hands. "I googled him."

Tammy hid her grin. "How naughty of you."

Jessie uncovered her face, her eyes round. "Not like that.

230

Not that I know exactly what you mean, but I looked him up. Oh, he's just so…"

"Jessie, come on. We're surrounded by gods among men every single day. Haven't you grown immune?"

Jessie clicked her tongue. "Have you?"

Tammy let her smile show. "Touché. However, today's meeting is all about the new builder. Let's just try to focus on what he's bringing to Cypress. Take notes. That should keep you busy."

"Yes." Jessie brightened. "Oh, yes! I love to take notes."

"There you go."

"You know Ben will be there, too," Jessie added.

Tammy nodded. "Since he's the architect on the project, that shouldn't be a surprise."

"But you'll have to sit there. With him. So close."

"What are you getting at?"

Jessie waved a hand. "There's electricity between you two. And maybe more. Lettie Fairfax says—"

Tammy held up a hand. "And let me stop you right there. Don't allow Lettie into your head, Jessie."

"But she's always right. What if she sees that I want this new guy?"

"Do you?" Tammy raised her brows. "Now, this is news."

Jessie blushed pink. "I don't want him. I mean, I don't know if I could want him. Or whatever."

"Pull yourself together before the meeting. Compile your own questions in case Rick calls for them and you'll be fine."

"But what about you and Ben?"

"What about me and Ben?" Tammy countered.

Jessie must have read the don't-go-there expression on Tammy's face, because she shook her head. "Okay, okay. No more talk about electricity. Or Lettie."

Tammy gave a short nod. "There's a good girl."

Jessie took in a deep breath, letting it out with a *whoosh*. "Thanks, Tammy. You're always so cool and calm in these situations."

"What situations?"

"Men and women stuff. Me? I'm a mess."

"Go make your lists, Jessie. Keep yourself busy until the meeting."

Jessie nodded again. "Thanks. I'll see you in there."

Tammy waved the girl out of her office and took a long sip of her now-just-right latte. Electricity, huh? Maybe Lettie was right there, but as for the rest of it? No way. She might have called a few matchups at Cypress in her time. But she was way off if she thought anything more than sexual magnetism drew Tammy to Ben.

As she scrolled through her phone to check her schedule, she pulled up the texts she'd sent Ben Friday night. Oh, she'd been out of her mind to put some of those things in virtual writing. He'd made good on just about everything she'd suggested, though. And then some.

Her phone dinged as a message arrived just then. She shouldn't have been surprised to see it was from Ben.

See you at the meeting. Lunch after?

Her heart gave a silly little flip at the invitation. This was dangerous. She'd known it going in and she'd gone in anyway. All the way in. And now he wanted to date?

"Oh, what the heck," she murmured, texting him back an acceptance.

Electricity? Oh, yeah. All kinds of electricity. Followed by a lunch date, though?

She had to be very careful or she'd fall right into the trap she'd been trying to avoid since the second she'd clapped eyes on him.

Forever.

Chapter 17

Ben sat on Tammy's couch, sticking a fork into the best damn lasagna he'd ever tasted. Tammy sat cross-legged beside him, holding her own plate. She wore his Henley and a pair of panties and nothing else. The shirt was way too big, and gapped nicely in front and draped off of one shoulder. Her hair was loosely braided and she didn't have any makeup on. She was gorgeous.

"You made this," he said again, letting out a groan. "Seriously."

She flushed a little, but that might be from the fact that he'd given her too many orgasms to count upstairs in her bed.

"Yep. With my own sauce, too," she said with pride in her voice. "You should have tasted it when it was hot."

"Maybe." He eyed her. "But first I wanted to taste something else that was hot."

She laughed softly and shook her head at him.

They'd just spent the last hour doing the hottest things to each other and he was wrung dry. It was a great way to spend a Friday night.

"You outdid yourself up there, Big Ben."

234

Her voice was husky, probably from all those delicious moans and groans he'd gotten out of her tonight.

"Tamara, you turned me inside out."

She smiled, taking up another bite of lasagna. "You'd think that after two weeks we'd get bored."

"I'm an architect, honey. I see all the angles and logistics. Load-bearing possibilities and stress points."

"Ooh, I love it when you talk dirty," she teased.

He laughed. This was new for him. Hanging around and eating what a woman cooked for him. Laughing and teasing long after they were both satisfied.

"So, what are you up to this weekend?" he asked.

She arched one brow, her body going a little rigid. "Why?"

"Ty and Cassie are having a party tomorrow night. At his place in the village. Something about celebrating the start of their life together."

"Didn't we do that at their wedding?" She shrugged. "Oh, I can't blame them. But I don't think I'll go to the party, thanks."

He shifted on the couch to face her. "Why not?"

"Because going to that party with you would be very date-y, Ben."

"We are dating, Tammy."

235

She sat up straighter. "No. We're not."

He set his scraped-clean plate on the coffee table and crossed his arms. "Then what do you call what we're doing?"

She shrugged that one bare shoulder. "Having fun?"

"Is that a question?"

"Aren't you having fun?"

He smiled, slow and easy. "Hell, yeah. But we go out, too. In my book, that's dating."

"Maybe." Her brows drew together. "I haven't dated much."

"I find that really hard to believe. You're freaking gorgeous and a fantastic time."

That got a smile out of her. "Thanks. Back atcha." She ran her gaze over him. "Have you dated a lot?"

"Not a lot, no. I was always more of a one- or two-night kind of guy."

Her gaze slid away. "I don't believe that."

"Believe it or not, it's true. Before you, anyway."

Her head shot up, her eyes round. "Don't do that. Don't say anything you don't mean."

He held up his hands. "I only meant that you're the first woman I've spent more than a couple of nights with."

She slanted him a look, a smile just curving one corner of

her mouth. "I am pretty amazing."

He laughed, feeling on more solid ground. He'd come pretty close to saying words he'd never said before. Hell, he wasn't even sure he knew what love was. He was in no position to push any feelings on a girl even more relationship-leery than he was.

"So, will you come to the party with me?"

She appeared to think for a second, and then shook her head. "No. I don't want to give your family, and by family, I mean Claire, any ideas about a future between you and me."

He gave her a nod. "Okay. The offer stands, though. No strings."

She smiled, and for a split second he wished he could offer her more than what they had right now. That he could be a different guy than the one he'd always been.

Then she put her plate next to his and leaned into him and he let himself forget anything but the feel of her beneath his hands and the bliss of her mouth against his lips.

This was what they had. This was what he wanted. What they both wanted. Everything else was for everyone else.

When he got to Ty and Cassie's house on Saturday night, he was sure he'd made the right decision not to push Tammy for more. Who was he kidding? He wasn't a forever kind of guy, no matter what she might think. And what they had was fan-freaking-tastic. He could admit to himself that he missed having her here with him tonight, though.

"Hey, bro." Jake strolled up to him and handed him an opened bottle of beer. "You look like you could use a cold one."

"Thanks." Ben took a drink and lifted his chin toward his little sister. "Cassie looks pretty happy."

Jake grinned. "She does. Hurricane Bill blew back up to Boston right after the wedding, so I'm pretty happy, too."

"He didn't hang around. That's for sure."

"I didn't expect him to." Jake took a drink. "He never does."

"He never came out to California much," Ben said.

Jake looked at him in surprise. "Not even to disapprove of something? Hmm. Must have been nice."

"Nope. He came out for my high school graduation. I think that's the only time we saw him."

"Tell me your poor mother didn't carry a torch for that son-of-a-bitch."

Ben shook his head. "She didn't. I don't know how she ever got tangled up with him in the first place. She was so different."

"From him?"

"From a lot of people, actually. She was a free spirit. Kind of a hippy." Warmth warred with the hollow feeling he always got when he thought about his mother. He missed her, but he could remember her alive more now than he'd been able to before. "You know, the way Harmony describes her parents? That was my mom."

"I'm sorry you lost her." Jake's expression fell a little. "We lost our mom a long time ago but I still feel it."

"And we're left with Bill."

Jake shrugged. "Such is life. That's why I'm glad we're making our own lives separate from him."

"You are."

"And you're not?"

Ben scoffed. "Bill set this up, Jake. The whole thing."

"Maybe he got Forbes leaning in your direction, but that guy would never dance to Bill's tune."

Ben reasoned Mr. Forbes was truly excited about his contribution to the latest development. Last week, when he'd seen the Craftsman bungalow design Ben created, he'd been visibly pleased. It was pretty tough to fake that kind of enthusiasm, especially coming from a no-nonsense guy like Forbes.

"I guess that's true," Ben said.

Jake nodded and turned to the gathering, and Ben did likewise. "So why are you on your own tonight?"

"Why shouldn't I be?"

"Seems to me Tammy should be here with you."

Ben bristled a little. "We're not connected at the hip."

Jake chuckled. "That's not what I heard."

"Nice," Ben said with a small smile. "I meant that we're just taking it easy."

"So…no date on Saturday night?"

Ben didn't answer, but just drank more of his beer. Claire came up and hugged Jake's waist as her husband draped an arm over her shoulders.

"Hey, Ben." Claire tilted her head to the side. "Sorry Tammy couldn't make it tonight."

"Yeah. How do you know that, exactly?"

Claire blinked at him. "Because I called her this afternoon and she said she had plans."

"Did she?" This was news to him. "Huh."

Jake and Claire exchanged a look, and then Claire's cheeks turned pink. "She was going out, I think."

"Going out." Ben drank more of his beer. "Huh."

Jake and Claire didn't say more about Tammy and her busy

240

night. Going out, or whatever. Claire gave her husband a kiss and went off to where Cassie and Harmony were gathered in the kitchen with Ty's mother. She lived in Ty's house, which was why the newlyweds planned to continue the habit of staying out at the tent-cabin now and then. Like his sister told him, they needed their privacy and Ty's mother needed her independence.

"On your own tonight?" Rick asked him.

Ben huffed out a breath. "Yes. I'm on my own."

Rick pulled back. "Just making conversation, Ben."

Ben rubbed a hand over his face. "I know. Sorry."

"What's up with you?"

"Nothing." He drained his beer. "Nothing's up."

Rick nodded, and when Ben didn't add anything else to the conversation he made his way back to the couch where Jake and Ty were seated. Ben stood there, looking into his empty bottle. Tammy was busy. Tammy was going out.

He fished his phone out of his pocket and saw there weren't any cute or sexy texts from her, either.

"Where the hell is she?" he muttered.

***

Tammy finished painting polish on her pinkie toe just as a ringtone sounded from her cell beside her on the couch. It was a tinny rendition of Dean Martin's *Volare*, and signaled a call from Rosa Donato. The queen of the Shore. The Boss. In other words, her mother.

Taking a breath, Tammy picked up her phone and swiped to answer. "Hey, Mom."

"Tamara, why are you home?"

She took a breath, gathering the relaxation she'd only just been relishing. She wore her favorite well-worn long-sleeve T with her fuzzy pink pajama pants and her face was scrubbed clean of makeup. Her hair was pulled up in a ponytail and she was focused on chilling. At least she was, until her mother called.

"You called my cell," she finally said. "My mobile phone. How do you know I'm home?"

Her mother made her trademark snort/scoff. "A mother knows." Another trademark. "Why aren't you out with a man tonight?"

"Because I had plans." She winced, knowing her mother would see right through the excuse.

"Ha! You said you had plans but yet you're home painting your nails."

Tammy held the phone away from her ear for second to eye

the screen, and then brought it back. "How do you know these things? Never mind. A mother knows."

Her mother huffed. "I'm coming down there."

"What? Why?" Tammy sat up, holding the phone tighter to her ear. "Why are you coming down here? I thought Teresa was close to her time?"

"Your sister has four weeks to go before the baby will be born."

"Yeah, but she needs you there. A mother's care to help through this difficult time."

"Difficult time? Tell me, what does my independent, unattached daughter know about it?"

"Nothing." Thank God. "So Teresa is doing okay?"

"Yes, yes. It's the most natural thing in the world, having babies. Which you would know, if you ever found yourself a man."

"I've found plenty of men, Mom."

"I mean, the right man."

Ben popped into her head in that instant, scaring the crap out of her. "Okay." She dragged out the word. "Why are you coming down here again?"

"To check on you, Tamara."

243

"Come on, Mom. I don't need you checking up on me."

"Forgive me for caring about my daughter." Her tone was put-upon and classic Rosa Donato. "I just want to make sure you're doing all right."

"I'm fine. Believe me. Work is going great, and—"

"Pff, work. Yes, work. So I'll come down and you can show me around your Cypress Corners again. I'm sure it's change since I've been down there."

"It has. But what about Dad?"

"What about him? Your father is fine. He and your brother Gino and going to keep an eye on things while I'm gone. I'll only be there for three days."

Tammy rolled her eyes to the ceiling, and then let out a breath of resignation. "When are you getting here?"

"I'll be there Friday afternoon. I'll send you my itinerary on the email."

Tammy almost laughed at her mother's phrasing, but knew better. Rosa was coming into the techno age slowly but surely.

"I'll keep an eye out for it," Tammy said.

"You can pick me up?"

"Of course."

"Good!" Tammy could almost see her mother clasping her

hands in delight. "Make plans for us on the weekend, Tamara. Maybe we can cook a meal together for your friends."

Tammy said nothing to that.

"I'll say good night, then," her mother added.

"Good night, Mom."

Her mother signed off and Tammy set the phone back down on the couch cushion. Running her hands over her thighs, she puzzled over her mother's upcoming visit. It wasn't completely out of the blue. Rosa usually made a pilgrimage, as she called it, to see her wayward daughter at least twice a year. She insisted it bridged the time between Tammy's visits home which, Tammy could admit to herself, were less frequent than even her mother's visits.

She had to find a way out of the whole dinner-party thing somehow. Or maybe she could get away with inviting only Jake and Claire. Even if she wanted to include Ben, and he was the person she would want to include, what would her mother think? A gorgeous, single guy as a dinner guest? Jeez, the woman would be hearing wedding bells before her famous tiramisu was served.

Tammy picked up her phone again, so tempted to text Ben. But no, she'd promised herself that she would put some space between them. She could survive one Saturday night alone. He was with his family and she was on her own. Claire had pressed her, though. So Tammy had caved and told her she had plans. Plans with pajama pants and pink nail polish, but plans nonetheless.

She clicked the TV on and switched to one of the cooking channels. "If I'm having people over for dinner next Saturday, I better bring my A game or Mom will never let me hear the end of it."

Settling back, she studied her pretty pink toenails as the sounds of sizzling and chopping played in the background. Why hadn't she gone to the beach yesterday? That was her Friday thing. To head out to the coast and just chill. Ocean breezes and outdoor dining. No stress and no family. No Cypress either, when she was out there. It struck her then. She hadn't gone to the beach since Ben arrived in Cypress. What was up with that?

She knew just what was up with that. She liked spending time with him right here. Either in his room at the inn or at her townhouse. Seeing him at work. Catching lunch with him. Cooking for him, of all things. He made her laugh. He made her do a lot more, too.

Damn it, they were dating. And yet, she'd urged him to go

to his family gathering without her. There was no way she wanted anyone to get the idea that they were a couple. They weren't, despite what Claire and the rest of the Chapmans might think.

"Wine," she decided out loud.

She got up off the couch and went over to the kitchen to grab a glass and the bottle of pinot chilling in the fridge. As she poured, her doorbell rang. Leaving her glass with a little reluctance, she walked to the front door and peered through the peephole. Her heart began to race.

It was Ben.

Chapter 18

Opening the door, she stared at him. His hair was mussed and his expression set.

"Ben, what are you doing here?"

"Where did you go tonight?" he bit out.

"Huh?"

"Your plans." He walked into the living room, running his fingers through his hair which explained its condition. "You told Claire you were going out."

She closed the front door and leaned back against it, crossing her arms. "You're jealous," she marveled aloud.

His head jerked as he turned to face her. "What?"

Warmth spread through her. This was new. For the two of them, yeah. But also just for her.

"You, Ben Chapman, are jealous."

He gaped, and then let his hands fall to his sides. "I was just curious."

She snorted. "Okay. Well, I didn't go anywhere. I just told Claire I was going out to get her off my back."

The hopeful expression on his face was adorable and more than a little hot. "Yeah?"

"Look at me." She gestured over her outfit. "Do I look like I'm dressed for a night out?"

His gaze was hot on her and she suddenly remembered she never wore a bra with her favorite long-sleeve shirt.

"You look like you're dressed for a night in," he said.

"Yep." She pushed off the door. "And I just opened a bottle of wine. Want to join me?"

His smile was crooked but his eyes sparkled. She took this expression for what it was. He was a little bit embarrassed and a whole lot turned on.

"Oh, yeah."

He followed closely on her heels as she made her way back to the kitchen.

"Grab yourself a glass," she said, uncorking the bottle again. "It's a little sweet, but good for a Saturday night alone."

"But you're not alone." He deftly poured his own glass and raised it in a salute. "Not anymore."

"True." She took another sip, and then deliberately set her glass on the counter. "So, is this a bootie call?"

His brows raised. "No."

He really looked confused and adorable. And as hot as he'd ever looked. He wore dark jeans and one of those Henley shirts she loved with a couple of buttons undone. She couldn't help teasing him.

Placing her hands on her hips, she tilted her head. Her ponytail swung to one side. "Then you don't want any of this?"

His eyes darkened in a second. "I would never say that. Not on a bet."

Didn't that just make her feel good! She was a mess. Ratty clothes, tangled hair. No makeup. The hunger on his face told her none of that matter.

Hiding the flush she could feel on her cheeks, she drank more of her wine. She set her glass down again, taking a breath.

"So where does this leave us?" she asked him.

"I'm thinking upstairs." His glass was beside hers as he came closer. "Or downstairs. Or on the stairs. At the moment, I'm not very particular."

She reached up and pulled out her ponytail holder, shaking her head as she watched him watching her. "I'm not sure, Ben. I'm pretty tired."

He wrapped his arms around her, nuzzling her neck. "Yeah?"

"Mmm hmm." She leaned away from his magical mouth and sighed. "I planned a quiet night."

He growled softly. "Quiet night? Not when I do what I want to you."

She shivered. "And what's that, exactly?"

His smile was smooth and sexy. "I'm going to taste you until you scream."

His hands were on her, cupping her breasts. Her nipples tightened almost painfully as she held on to his arms. "Ben."

"Hmm?" He was nuzzling her again, his cheeks rough and his mouth hot. "Tell me what you want now."

"This." She gasped as he sucked her breast through her thin shirt. "More of this."

He grabbed her beneath her butt like he had that first night after the wedding, carrying her only far enough to drop her on the couch. Shoving her shirt up and out of the way, he licked and sucked at her flesh until she was sobbing. Her stretchy pants were the next to go and he stopped to kiss her toes.

"Pink." He licked the sole of her foot. "I like it."

He had her panties off and his lips and fingers were doing all sorts of things that made her sigh and moan. "Please, Ben."

He shifted to hold himself up on one arm as he came up to kiss her. "Please, what?"

She sat up and pulled at his shirt until he was deliciously

bare-chested. "Please me."

"I will, Tamara." His voice was rough and scraped against her in the best way. "I will."

He toed off his shoes and began to unbutton his jeans. She wanted him all over her. Kissing her. Touching her. Wanted so bad for him to come into her that she was nearly frantic. She took a long minute to catch her breath, though.

He was cut, and she would never get tired of looking at him. She traced those hot little dents on either side of his hips with her fingers, and his butt was firm beneath her hands.

He tipped his head back, his breath coming fast. "Tammy, you're killing me."

She pulled him down on top of her, snaking one hand between them to cup him. He was hard. He was hot. He was what she wanted right now.

"Come on, Big Ben."

He growled again and moved until he was almost inside of her. "This is going to be fast."

"Fast is good." She closed her eyes, arching as his hands moved over her breasts and belly down to where she so desperately needed him. "Now," she gasped. "Please."

He pushed inside her. Deep. She cried out, her climax

teasing just out of reach. Moving as fast as he'd promised, she gripped him as he touched every bit of her. Peeking open one eye, she saw him staring down at her. His expression was intense and his eyes dark. That did it. She lost herself in the next second, coming again and again as she let loose with a scream.

He kept it up, moving harder and faster as she nearly cried. It felt so good, losing herself with him. When he came, deep inside of her, she held on tight as she rode every shudder and shake of his big body.

He collapsed with a breathy laugh, his body all ease and release. "Tammy, honey." He kissed her, still deep inside of her. "That wasn't very quiet."

She laughed with him, her arms dropping like stones to her sides as she opened her eyes to stare up at him. "You wore me out."

He brought his face to hers. "That's good to know." He kissed her, so tenderly she felt like crying. "That's also only the start."

She blinked her stinging eyes, focusing instead on how good she felt with the weight of him on her.

"Good bye, quiet night," she said.

He laughed again.

***

"Hey, Ben."

Ben looked up from his drafting table to see Noah, the new builder, leaning into his office.

"Hey, Noah."

"I wondered if you wanted to head out to the site with me."

"Sure. What's up?"

"They're marking off the lot for the model. The Craftsman."

Ben nodded. "Yeah, I saw that in the schedule."

"Well, I want to walk it and wondered if you wanted to come with me."

"Sounds good." Ben kicked off his shoes and stepped into the work boots he kept in the office. "So you're a hands-on kind of guy, too?"

"I don't mind getting dirty."

Noah's words shouldn't have made him think about Tammy, but they did. Saturday night had been more fun than he'd had in a long time. He had a hard time getting that bit of fun out of his head over the past five days. She'd look so soft and touchable in her little pink pajamas. And when she'd told him she really didn't have plans with any other guy, something shifted inside him. Something that made him want to hold her

254

and never let go.

Tying his laces, he refocused. He straightened and took his tablet from his desk, lifting his chin in the direction of the breakroom.

"Let's grab a couple of waters and head over there," he said, putting aside Tammy and all they'd done on that not-very-quiet night before he found himself in a bad way today.

He passed her office on the way out and saw her desk was vacant. She must be out on a tour. Since Saturday night, it seemed like they'd turned a corner. She'd stayed home on a Saturday night and he'd admitted he'd been jealous when he thought she hadn't. So he guessed that meant they were dating. Damn, he'd never really dated before. He hadn't been kidding when he'd told Tammy that.

He and Noah rode out to the site in one of the golf carts kept charged and ready to go during business hours. Noah drove and Ben held onto the canopy support and leaned back.

"So how do you like Cypress so far?" he asked Noah.

"I really like it," Noah answered. "The scenery is pretty, and I don't just mean the landscape."

Ben tamped down a jab of protectiveness. "Yeah."

"I know a few of them are taken, but still." Noah winked. "It doesn't hurt to look, right?"

Ben eyed him as he steered the golf cart. The guy was good looking, in a surfer kind of way. That was funny, since Ben was a surfer and didn't look anything like this golden guy.

"No. It doesn't."

Noah didn't seem to catch Ben's tone, but he did change the subject. "So how is it, working with so much of your family?"

"I like it." He realized that was more than true. "My brothers are pretty cool."

"You get to see them a lot, then? Outside of work?"

Ben nodded in answer. Yeah, he did. Not that he behaved as though he liked it Saturday night. He'd brushed off one brother and snapped at another one. He really wasn't good at this family stuff.

They came to the site of the first model. The ground he'd seen with Tammy was now churned a rich, dark brown and had been rough-graded. There were a few trucks parked along the newly-paved street in front, and Noah's guys were pacing off the property lines.

Ben knew the infrastructure had been completed a couple of months ago, well before he was brought in on the project. Streetlights, water and utilities. Now, with the streets graded and some of them paved, he could envision the neighborhood even more clearly.

Noah parked the cart and Ben stepped out. As soon as his boots hit the pavement, that excitement gripped him again. This was his project. He could see the Craftsman smack dab in the middle of all that rough dirt. Plantings strategically placed to compliment the structure and still fall in line with what the Cypress Institute preferred. He scratched his chin.

"Noah, have you spoken with Harmony about the plants?"

Noah nodded. "Yep. The landscape at her and Rick's house is a great example of what we can do with native plants."

"Yeah. Tammy's townhouse, too. I couldn't name the plants out front but they go really well with the façade."

Noah's brows shot up. "You've been to Tammy's townhouse?"

Ben wouldn't make light of what he and Tammy were, even if he didn't really know right now. He sure wouldn't brush off Noah's question when the guy was already talking about the "scenery" at the office.

"Yes," he said.

Noah stilled, and then gave a slow nod. "Message received."

Ben shrugged. "I thought everyone knew we were dating."

257

"I think that Lettie woman might have said something."
Noah chuckled. "Actually, what she said I'm a little embarrassed
to repeat. Not about you, though. About me."

Ben rolled his eyes. "Yeah, she's something else. Did she
squeeze your arm?"

Noah's eyes went round. "Yes."

Ben grinned. "Be careful, man. She'll be trying to fix you up
with somebody soon."

"If I could get as lucky as you? I just might let her."

Ben didn't say anything more. What he had with Tammy
was so different from anything he'd ever experienced. They
were dating. He'd admitted that to himself and, finally, to other
people. Lucky? He was that. He was one lucky bastard to have
her want him as much as he wanted her.

One of Noah's guys called out, waving them over. Ben put
thoughts of luck and Tammy out of his head and followed the
builder over the sandy ground. He would just enjoy what he and
Tammy shared right now. That was all she wanted. He'd be a
moron if he let himself think they were anything more.

Again, he thought about how sweet and vulnerable she'd
looked there on the couch Saturday night. After he'd sent her to
the vaulted ceilings and brought her back down in his arms.

Stopping with Noah at one of the stakes marking the southeast corner of the lot, he nodded as Noah made introductions all around. Then he turned and faced where the house itself would be. Once the lot lines were marked, the next would be to plot out the concrete slab foundation for the house itself. That was what Ben was waiting for. To work with Noah and make sure all the materials he'd specified would be utilized. The Institute had signed off on Ben's selections and Noah seemed to be as dedicated to the spirit of the project as Ben was.

This wasn't the biggest or most important house he'd ever designed. It wasn't the most expensive or the most influential. No. It was a house that would be a home. An environmentally-conscious, state-of-the-art home with all the conveniences prospective homeowners look for when they come to Cypress, true. But it would also be a home where a family could grow in a place where they could learn and play and just be.

He nodded at something one of Noah's guys was saying, his mind on the fictional family and the not-yet-built Craftsman. Thick, squared-off columns holding a deep roof over the front porch. Recycled planking for the decking and stone facing created out of repurposed materials.

He suddenly pictured Tammy on the front porch, maybe

sipping iced tea or reading a book. Relaxing after work in a swing like the one on his brother Rick's front porch. God, he wanted to join her in that swing. Just chill and talk about the day as the late-afternoon light waned.

He froze. What the hell? He was picturing himself in that scene? Among all that domestic bliss he'd seen but never, ever wanted?

Christ. He had to get his head back in the game and play by her rules. Their rules, really. Before he started wanting more than she was prepared give. The thing was, he was tired of playing the game. He had to tread carefully, though. Tammy was as relationship-phobic as he'd ever been.

He knew one thing for sure as he stood there, picturing that future. He wanted more.

He wanted it all.

Chapter 19

Tammy drove slowly up the Arrivals ramp at the Orlando International Airport, bracing herself for the whirlwind that was Rosa Donato. She'd told Ben her mother was coming to town, but that was it. He had to know she wasn't going to be available for playdates for a while. Sneaking out wasn't an option under her mother's eagle eye. And sneaking Ben in wasn't going to happen, either.

She'd left the subject of a dinner party over the weekend completely out of their conversation. Why drag him into her family dynamic? And yes, even though it was only her mother who was visiting, the woman brought the whole Donato dynamic with her in her carry-on luggage.

The airport was just about the closest thing to Cypress Corners, sitting about a half hour or so to the northwest of the property. She could count on traffic heading into the airport to be heavy on a Friday afternoon, though. Today she didn't consider this a big problem as she followed the crawling line up to the long and winding curbside.

She spotted her mother in front of one of the wide glass doors in the Arrivals lane, standing under a different number than she'd texted but that wasn't surprising. Her mother probably came out under the number five liked she'd indicated but had seen someone to talk to under the seven. In fact, an older couple stood with her now. Their smiles were evident even as Tammy approached, a testament to her mother's warmth and way with people. Tammy had to give it to her. She might be a nudge with her family, and Tammy in particular, but everyone who met her fell instantly in love.

Pulling her convertible to a stop right next to the little group, she left the engine running and stepped out. "Hey, Mom."

Her mother turned, her face wreathed with a bright smile. "Tamara!"

Looking at her was like looking at a mirror set on twenty years in the future. Rosa wore her hair scraped back from her face with a wide hairband and her makeup was perfectly applied. Her mouth was a little wide and her eyes tilted up at the corners, and the combination made her still turn heads at fifty-five. That gave Tammy a sense of security. Her older sister might look like Dad but Tammy was the spit and image of Rosa.

Her mother hugged her tight, planting loud kisses on her cheek. Tammy welcomed the warm greeting, feeling a shift in her chest. She'd missed her mother. Who knew?

Rosa turned back to the couple. "This is my daughter. She's single."

"She's as pretty as you said, Rosa," the woman said.

Tammy gave them a tight smile. "Thank you. Mom, I can't leave the car here."

Her mother waved a hand. "I know, I know. I just wanted to introduce you to Paula and Stan Berkowitz. Their son Steven works in Orlando."

"He's a lawyer," Steven's proud mother declared.

Tammy wasn't impressed. Florida had over one hundred thousand attorneys, and Orlando had the lion's share of them if all the commercials that ran on TV were any indication.

"Nice to meet you." Tammy turned to her mother and grabbed her bright pink polka-dotted hard-shelled suitcase.

She fit it easily into her car's small trunk. At least her mother traveled light in the luggage department. Guilt and pressure were a whole other issue.

"Let's head to Cypress, Mom."

Her mother clasped her hands together. "Cypress! Paula, my daughter is the top salesperson at Cypress Corners. The place is just lovely. You have to come out to see it."

Paula and Stan exchanged a look of interest. "Maybe we

will."

"Look for my Tamara at the Sales Center."

"Okay, let's go." Tammy smiled at the couple again and urged her mother into the car.

"Yes, yes. Good bye, Paula. Stan. Look me up on the Facebook!"

Tammy closed her eyes with a sigh and got back behind the wheel. She'd left the air on but she suddenly felt very hot. A wave a nausea struck her. Holding tight to the wheel, she slowly took in a breath and blew it out.

"What's wrong?" her mother asked.

Tammy turned to her as the feeling left as quickly as it had come. "Nothing."

She shifted and pulled out into the ever-present procession of cars through the Arrival lane. She could feel her mother's eyes on her as they left the congestion of the airport and headed past ranches and farms on their way toward Cypress.

"I'm fine, Mom," she assured her.

"Pff." Her mother's usual sound of disagreement met Tammy's ears. "Something's wrong."

Tammy just shook her head. She'd eaten the fish sandwich special at the tavern for lunch today, but it hadn't seemed off.

She felt pretty okay at the moment, too. Maybe her stomach was queasy because of the intrusive woman seated next to her.

"So what would you like to do while you're here, Mom?"

"We're having a dinner party."

"I know. That's one evening. What about the other three days?"

Her mother waved a hand, flashing the familiar wedding ring set on her left hand. Tammy smiled at the memory those rings brought back to her. They sure could sting when you earned a swat on the butt, all right.

"Anything you think to do is fine with me, sweetheart," her mother said.

"Maybe shopping up in Orlando?"

"That sounds good. Are you seeing anyone?"

Tammy almost missed the stop sign on that swift change of subject. Making a show of waiting to drive forward, she let the silence stretch thin.

"Tamara, are you seeing anyone?" her mother asked again.

Tammy shook her head. "No one serious," was all she would answer.

Her belly twisted. She was serious about Ben, in a way. He was the only guy she wanted and she thought about him both in and out of bed. He was fun and gorgeous and such a good guy. A real Chapman, which she found both attractive and terrifying.

"Then you are seeing someone," her mother stated with a nod. "Good. He'll come to dinner tomorrow night."

Tammy knew that arguing would be futile. Rosa Donato didn't give an inch. She nodded, hopefully setting the entire discussion aside.

She soon steered into the entrance of Cypress Corners. A long drive bracketed by white ranch fencing and tall leafy trees led them into the center of town. The look of the place never failed to please her. She'd lived here for nearly five years, and still hadn't grown tired of it. It was quaint and pretty and felt like home.

"The trees have gotten so tall," her mother said.

Tammy flicked her eyes upward as she stopped at the sign in front of the Sales Center. "I guess they have. It's hard to tell when you walk under them every day."

Continuing on to the townhouse, she waved hello to a few of her neighbors out in the late September afternoon. Twilight was coming, and the sky was taking on that purple cast she loved.

"Look at you," her mother said. "You feel at home here."

"I really do." Tammy sounded surprised even to her own

ears. "It's my home."

"It's a nice place, Tamara. I'd prefer you someplace near your father and me, but I understand why you like it here."

Tammy clicked the garage open and parked the car, and then faced her mother. "Wow. That's the first time you've said that."

Her mother smiled. "I might be stubborn but I'm not blind. Besides, maybe this 'no one serious' might become Mister Right."

Ben *was* right. All kinds of right, but not what she wanted. Again, she felt like she was lying to herself. She was getting too comfortable having him around, and that could only be trouble.

"Come on inside, Mom." She and her mother and the bright pink polka-dot suitcase went on into the house. "How about I order us a pizza for dinner?"

Her mother's eyes went round. "Pizza? In Florida?"

Tammy laughed. "The guy who makes the pies at the tavern is from New York. It's pretty close to what you'd expect."

The woman didn't look convinced, but she nodded anyway. "All right, then."

Tammy ordered the pizza and helped her mother get settled in the spare bedroom upstairs. Dinner would be good. She had no worries about that. The conversation, though? There was no way her mother would drop the subject of men and dating. And now she had to invite Ben to dinner.

What would he think, coming to dinner to meet her mother? She just hoped he didn't jump to the conclusion that she was pushing for anything more than what they had going right now. That would lead to drama and, possibly, the end.

She so wasn't ready for this to be over.

***

Ben sat on the terrace of the inn on Sunday morning, much like he had on his very first Sunday morning in Cypress Corners. And like that first Sunday morning? He'd woken up alone. It sucked.

Tammy's mother was visiting. He'd never been the kind of guy a woman brings home to mom. That's for sure. Not that mothers didn't love him. They did. Not in a cougar kind of way but a "I have just the girl for you" way.

Clients were always inviting him to their homes after they moved into the house he'd designed for them. Their families were always there, celebrating and warming the houses. He'd endured a few fix-ups on those occasions, too. Sprung on him out of nowhere. He never encouraged it and never saw the

268

women in question again no matter how attractive they might have been. It was too messy to get involved, even for one night, with someone connected to a client. Hell, getting involved at all could be a major pain in the ass.

When Tammy had called him last night, he'd counted an entirely different kind of invitation. She'd started their short conversation by telling him her mother was visiting, and that she was having a few people over for dinner and wanted to include him as one of the party. Her voice had been clipped, and he correctly guessed from the jump that her mother had probably been within earshot.

His brothers and sister, and their spouses, had been there too. As much as he liked his siblings, he couldn't deny that the whole evening had a very domestic feel to it. He'd managed to avoid anything domestic for the whole of his adult life. This was different, though. Tammy was different.

The food was terrific, and made by both Tammy and her mother. Tammy's killer lasagna and some kind of Italian bread that was so crusty yet soft he'd eaten about ten pieces. He'd been able to keep from contributing much to the conversation that way too, and didn't feel guilty about that in the least.

Her mother was a force of nature. That was clear. Tammy

looked a lot like her, and seeing Mrs. Donato was like getting a glimpse of what Tammy would look like in twenty years. Nothing scary there. Tammy would be a knock-out long into her fifties, too.

The thing was, it was clear that Tammy's mother was pushing for Ben to date Tammy. If the woman only knew what Ben and Tammy had done all over that townhouse, she'd know she didn't have to worry about Tammy finding a guy. She'd found him, and what they had was pretty damn terrific.

What he felt for her, though? What he'd realized only two days ago was pretty damn scary, too. He had to talk to her. Alone. To ask if she was up for seeing where this was going. For real. He'd never said those things to another woman. Never suggested taking anything past the here and now. He couldn't have that conversation with an audience, and definitely not around her mother.

His eyes strayed to the stretch of beach near the lake. The loungers were empty this morning. Tammy was probably tied up with her mother's visit today. He thought she'd told him that the woman was heading back up north tomorrow, so maybe he could man up and talk to Tammy after that.

His cell rang and he glanced at the screen. Jake. Smiling, he answered.

"Hello."

"Hey, bro," Jake said. "What are you up to today?"

"Nothing." Nothing with Tammy, anyway. "Why?"

"Barbeque over at Rick's today. You in?"

"I guess."

There was a long pause. "You don't sound like yourself."

"Who do I sound like?"

"I don't know. You sound a little...distracted."

"I am." Before Jake could wheedle a reason out of him, he went on. "The first house is set to break ground."

"I heard. Congrats, bro. You've been working your ass off."

"I have." Ben took in a breath. "What time?"

"One o'clock. I'll tell Harmony to expect you."

"Thanks. See you then."

He disconnected and stared out a the lake again. Ripples of water caught the sunlight, and the effect was nice. Relaxing. He could see himself settling here, too. Damn, he had to get his shit together.

"One step at a time, man," he told himself.

Rising, he went back to his room to dress for a run along the lakeshore. To clear his head. If he planned on talking to Tammy about the future he better make sure he brought his balls with him to the table.

By the time Monday came around, he was ready to hit something. His skin felt too tight and he had to keep catching his breath. Thankfully he'd lost himself in a new house design at the office, which killed a few hours. Tammy wasn't in the Sales Center this morning, since she'd had to take her mother back to the airport. He had this information from Claire, who'd filled him in on Tammy's itinerary yesterday at Rick and Harmony's. He'd listened closely, too. He didn't even care if Jake shot him a smug expression when he caught him.

He heard the sound of Tammy's voice when she walked into the Sales Center, and his lungs seized a little. He had it bad.

Coming deliberately to his feet, he casually made his way to the breakroom. It was as good a time as any for a coffee break, wasn't it?

Jessie sat at one of the tables, and her blond brows shot up as she looked from Ben to Tammy and back again. Tammy hadn't seen him yet, so he looked his fill. She wore her usual outfit, tight in all the right places while still crisp. She did something to him in those clothes. Made him want to get her all wrinkled.

"Hey, Ben," Jessie squeaked.

The girl was always a little bit flustered, and he couldn't figure out why. Noah had mentioned something about that, too.

"Hey, Jessie."

Tammy turned, letting her eyes run over him in that way she had. "Good morning."

He blinked. She sounded off. Clipped, again. Maybe it was being around her mother all weekend. Like she'd picked up a bit of up-north in her voice. He dismissed that idea in the next second. Her mother sounded like she was born and bred at the Jersey shore, and Tammy didn't draw out her words or drop her R's even a little.

"Did your mother get off okay?" he asked.

She nodded, and then turned away to fuss with the coffee maker. Her movements were smooth but he didn't miss the stiffness in her shoulders. He shot a look at Jessie, who grabbed her coffee cup and headed past him.

"See you later," she rushed out as she left him alone in the breakroom with Tammy.

"Sure," he returned absently.

He walked over to Tammy, where she was staring at the coffee maker as it effortlessly brewed her cup. "You don't have

273

to watch it, you know."

She flattened her palms on the counter. "I wasn't."

Stepping close behind her, he leaned in. "I missed you this weekend," he said softly.

Her rigidity seemed to grow. "Oh?"

"I can't wait to make up for lost time."

He heard her suck in a breath as she finally turned to face him. Her body skimmed over his in the best way even as she leaned away from him.

"I don't know if I can."

"If you can what?"

"Come over."

"Then I'll come to your place," he suggested.

She placed a hand on his chest, scorching him even as her expression stayed cool. "I don't think…" Her brow furrowed as she started to move her hand in a caress. "Sure. Your place, I think. That's fine."

"Good. I'll grab us some takeout from the tavern. Burgers okay?"

She shrugged, and then nodded. He touched her chin, tipping her face up to his. He wanted to kiss her and wipe away that little pout.

"What's wrong?" he asked instead.

"Nothing's wrong." Her smile was a little too bright. "I just have a lot of work to catch up on today."

She moved quickly away from him, running her fingers through her hair before tossing it over her shoulder. He'd seen that move before. It was her trademark and he thought that right now she was using it as a diversion. Just what was she hiding?

Pressing her hand to her belly, she took a breath and straightened. "I'll see you later then."

With that, she breezed out of the room.

"Okay," he said into the space she'd left behind.

Chapter 20

How was she going to get through this day?

Tammy and her mother had a surprising heart-to-heart Saturday night, and she'd had to admit her growing feelings for Ben. While her mother was over the moon in the most obvious way, Tammy had to talk her back down to earth. Her relationship with Ben had her confused, to put it mildly. And yesterday morning when she'd felt like crap again? Her mother hadn't missed it. That was for sure.

Tammy couldn't blame the wine she'd had Saturday night. She hadn't had any because she just hadn't felt like it. Sweet tea was the unofficial drink of the south, so she'd just drunk that with dinner. She'd been so nervous having Ben over to meet her mother that she'd sure as heck wanted to keep her faculties clear.

And just why was she feeling like crap, then? Her mother had nailed it on the first try, coming up with an answer that never would have even occurred to Tammy.

Her eyes stung with tears and she gave in to them for the first time in a very long time. Propping her elbows on her desk, she buried her face in her hands. What the hell was she going to do?

A soft rapping came at her door, and she immediately dismissed the idea that it was Ollie. Thank God. He would guess what was wrong in a hot minute and she didn't want to hear his I-told-you-so right now.

Grabbing up a tissue from the box set on a shelf behind her, she dabbed at her eyes and cleared the thickness from her throat.

"Yes?" she called.

The door opened and Claire poked her head in. "Hey, there." Claire's eyes went round. "What's wrong?"

Tammy tossed the tissue into the small trash can under her desk. "Nothing." She smiled. "Nothing's wrong."

Jeez, was she going to have to say that all day?

Claire clicked her tongue and came fully into the office, shutting the door tight behind her. "Something's wrong. Is it Ben?"

Tammy shook her head. "No. Ben's fine." She thought back to his leaning close like he'd wanted to kiss her. "He's perfect."

"Then tell me what's bothering you, Tammy. You can tell me anything."

She stared into Claire's big blue eyes and felt her heart give a sorry thump. She could tell her anything? How could she tell Claire, her best friend, that the very thing she and her husband

277

have been trying to achieve for months now had just fallen unwanted into her lap?

She couldn't. Not right now. This was all too new, and it began right at the moment her mother stated what should have been obvious to Tammy.

"It's nothing, Claire," she lied. "I guess having my mother here was just a little overwhelming."

She risked a glance out the window to make sure there were no gray clouds in the sky. No sign of lightning. Maybe God wouldn't strike her down for lying and for blaming her mother.

Claire's brows drew together, and then she smiled a little. "My mother has been gone for so long I'd forgotten the particular set of skills they can have."

Tammy nodded, feeling worse by the moment. "So you get it."

"Oh, yeah. My mom was good at the guilt. Whenever I said anything less-than-nice about my dad she got right on me."

Claire's dad had a gambling problem that still dogged him. He kept a lid on it with his daughter's help, but it was a problem that would never really go away.

Claire stood. "I'll let you decompress, then. Maybe we can go to yoga tomorrow? I know I could use a stretch."

"Sure. Sounds good."

Claire patted Tammy's shoulder, making her feel like a piece of crap all over again, and left the office. Damn, that was really cruddy. Tammy had no choice, though. Claire and Jake were trying so hard for a baby and now it seemed that she would be the one with the newest little Chapman.

Leaning back in her chair, she eyed her belly. It was so hard to wrap her head around all of this. She was pregnant? What the hell? How had that happened?

Yes, she and Ben had been together too many times to count. It didn't matter that they'd only known each other for a little over a month. Even though she'd tried so hard to keep him in the friend zone for half that time, they'd more than made up for that when she'd finally admitted to herself that she had to have him.

"So much for making a decision and sticking with it," she grumbled to herself.

She'd never wanted to give in to what had been between them from the second she'd met him. That made her think about her vow to never make a commitment. She didn't want the family thing. She didn't even want a boyfriend, for God's sake. And now a great big family thing—okay, a teeny-tiny family thing but still—was staring her in the face.

She couldn't tell Ben. She knew just what he'd do if he found out. He was a friggin' Chapman, after all. Forever and family was all over him no matter what he might say to the contrary. Just look at Rick and Jake. Rick had been as free-wheeling as Jake had been, if not as upfront about it. Yet now they were both tried-and-true family men. That struck her hard in the chest. All Jake needed was the family.

Ben would push for them to stay together for good. A chill ran through her. She never stayed for good. Not once. She seemed to be missing that gene. All the other Donatos made that family stuff work but she'd never had even the slightest temptation to try it on for size with any of the guys she'd gone out with. Or fooled around with, for that matter. Ben would want forever and she just wasn't built that way.

Here she sat, virtually on the nest. She didn't know what she was going to do about her little ravioli. The nickname her mother had used for the coming baby made her smile. A warmth spread through her and her eyes pricked again.

"Jeez, hormones are a real bitch," she whispered, reaching for another tissue.

How could she rationally think about her future when she

was brewing and bubbling inside?

Ben wanted her to come over tonight, and if she was a stronger woman maybe she could resist the lure. She'd tried. Oh, how she'd tried. In the end, she couldn't. No matter how much she should put some distance between them, she didn't want that distance tonight. No. Tonight she'd have him every way she wanted him. And afterwards?

Afterwards, she'd say good bye and make it stick.

***

Ben opened the bottle of wine he'd bought at the little market in the town center, setting it and two glasses on the small table near the fireplace. Something was bothering Tammy, and maybe a little bit of vino would help her relax enough to tell him what was going on.

They hadn't agreed on a time, but he figured she'd come by around seven. He grabbed the big bag from the tavern and put the takeout boxes near the wine bottle. The salty, earthy smell of burgers and fries filled his guest room. He rooted around in the bag and set the napkins and plastic silverware on the table too and stepped back.

"This feels a whole lot like a date," he muttered.

That didn't matter. She was coming here and he would talk

281

to her about moving forward. To see if what they had could be something more, as un-freaking-believable as that should be.

A knock came at the door. "Ben?" she asked. "It's me."

Heat brushed over him at the sound of her voice. He crossed to the door and opened it. Damn, she looked good. Tight jeans and a snug knit shirt hugged her body and her hair was down and swept forward over one shoulder. Her face, though. She wore an expression he'd never seen from her before. She looked a little scared.

"What's wrong?" he asked.

She blinked, and then gave him a smile that seemed a little brittle. "Nice to see you, too."

He took her hand and pulled her into the room. "Sorry. It's nice to see you." His gaze ran over. "Very nice."

She shrugged. "It's fall. Not quite jeans weather, but I was tired of waiting for Cypress to catch up with the calendar."

He closed the door behind her. "Yeah, I get you. I used to do the same thing in California. When autumn leaves made out of paper are the only sign that the season changed, we take it where we can."

She eased a bit. "Like in a pumpkin spice latte."

He wrapped his arms around her. "You like those." He

kissed her, and her lips clung for a split second as he pulled back. "Spicy and sweet, like you."

She placed a hand on his chest. "Easy there, Big Ben. I believe you promised me dinner?"

He placed a hand on his belly and bowed. "Burgers. From the tavern."

Her face brightened. "Oh, good. I'm starving."

They sat down and the mood eased a little more as they began to eat.

He picked up the wine bottle, holding it over the glass in front of her. Her hand shot out to cover the glass. "No, thanks."

Lifting the bottle away, he set it back on the table. "Okay. Do you want a soda? Water?"

"A water would be great."

He grabbed a bottle of water and cracked it open for her, pouring it into her wine glass.

She thanked him again and nibbled on a French fry. "I just feel like I need some detox."

"And a burger and fries is a way to do that?"

She smiled. "I said 'some,' Ben. Fries are a crucial food group."

He agreed to that. As he fed one appetite, he couldn't wait to feed another. He craved her, sitting there doing nothing but innocently eating her meal, and wanted to lick the salt off her lips. Taste the sweetness of her skin. Feel her come around him before giving in to his own climax.

"Enough," he said, pushing aside his empty box. "You done?"

She looked up, still chewing, and nodded. "I'll nibble on these later."

"Mmm, nibble." He took her hand again, hauling her up against him. "I love the way you nibble."

She laughed deep in her throat, tossing her head back to stare up at him. "I love the way your mouth feels on me, too."

Lust tore through him and he sucked in a breath. "Tamara, I'm going to make you scream."

She seemed to hesitate, and then she got a glint of determination in her eyes. "Not if I make you scream first."

Her hands were wild on him and he helped her strip his clothes off. Pushing him down on the bed in only his boxer briefs, she stood back and smiled before quickly taking her own clothes off. He'd seen her body so many times now, but it never ceased to make him weak.

When he reached for her, she grabbed his hand.

"Not a chance, Ben. I'm driving, remember?"

She crawled over him, pushing him down onto his back. He let her take the lead, loving the way her body felt against his. She straddled his waist and he could feel her heat. He was so hard now he could barely breathe.

"Tammy, please," he urged. "I'm dying here."

Reaching behind her ass, she stroked him. The position thrust her breasts higher and his mouth watered. She moved and he felt her wet heat against the flesh of his lower belly. Her hands were on his chest now and his were in fists.

"I have to touch you," he rasped.

She bit her lip and shook her head, staring down at him. "Briefs, Ben." She moaned a little. "Off."

He reached down and shoved his briefs out of the way as she shifted. Before he could think to grab a condom, she slid down on him.

"Tammy, wait," he bit out.

She froze, and then climbed off of him and reached over to the nightstand. Then she was there again. Tight around him as she rode him hard.

He held on to her hips and let her have her way. It was freeing. It was incredible. It was everything she was. Wild and

285

sweet and so hot he had to close his eyes before he lost control.

"Ben," she breathed, her voice rising. "Oh!"

When she bucked above him, crying out, he arched off the bed to meet her. His climax was beyond anything he'd had before, going on and on as she continued to move over him.

She collapsed onto his chest and his arms wrapped snugly around her. Burying his face in her hair, he breathed in the scent of her and himself. That thing shifted in his chest again, his heart beating with hers.

"Stay, Tammy," he said.

She held herself over him, her face soft and gorgeous. "Stay?"

This wasn't how he wanted to broach the subject, but his orgasm-rattled brain apparently hadn't thought things through.

"I want this," he told her.

She blinked, her eyes going wide. "What?" Scrambling off of him, she sat with her knees drawn to her chest. "What, exactly, do you want?"

The blood was slowly getting back to his head, so he took a second to collect his thoughts. Her face was pale and she looked almost afraid.

"I want this, Tammy," he said. "What we have."

She shook her head. "No. I can't think about this now. Not today."

"Why not?"

Her eyes were shiny now. What the hell was going on with her?

"I told you before, Ben." She got out of his bed in a blur and starting putting on her underwear. "God, how could you do this?"

"Do what?" He stood and pulled on his briefs as she stepped into her jeans. "Where are you going?"

"Home." She buttoned her jeans and put her shirt on, pulling her hair up and out of it to fall down her back. "My house."

"Tammy, I want to talk about this." He took a breath. "About us."

She froze, her mouth agape. "Us? There's no us. You can't say there is. Just like that."

"Why the hell not?" He stalked over to her. "Tell me what's going on with you."

She shook her head. "No, Ben. Damn it, I knew this would happen."

He stood there in his underwear, equal parts confused and pissed off. "You knew *what* would happen? Look, the way I feel

287

about you. I—"

Her hand flew up to cover his mouth. "Don't say it." Her voice was frantic. "Words you don't mean, Ben. Don't say them."

He grasped her wrist, pulling her hand away from his mouth. "Maybe I do."

"Maybe?" She tilted her head to the side, a sad smile on her lips. "I can't do a maybe. Not now."

She grabbed a hold of the doorknob, and then turned back to him. "I'll see you around."

She was gone in the next second, leaving him staring at the door for a long minute. What the hell had just happened?

One minute they were in his bed, giving and taking everything until they both broke in the best way. The next he'd said he wanted what they had and she'd freaked the fuck out.

Pulling on his jeans, he ran his fingers through his hair and sat down on the edge of the bed. Had he read everything wrong? They were good together. In and out of bed. He wasn't asking her to marry him, for God's sake. He just wanted to see where they were going. To think about what they could be.

"What the fuck?" he grumbled.

He poured himself another glass of wine and drank deeply.

288

He thought for a second.

"She gave me an out. Again."

He hadn't listened when she'd said she didn't want to sleep with him weeks ago. That had lasted days that had felt like weeks, but they'd found themselves in something good. Something real.

He knew she felt something for him, too. Maybe this wasn't love, but he couldn't see himself with anybody else but her.

Whatever the hell was going on with her, he had no idea what it was. Or how to fix it.

So he drank some more wine and wouldn't think about it tonight.

Chapter 21

Tammy splashed cold water on her face and stared hard into the mirror. She looked a little pale, but at least her eyes weren't red this morning. She'd stopped crying sometime on Sunday afternoon. How she'd made it through the rest of the week, she had no idea. At least her work hadn't suffered. Experience and professionalism had saved her from mucking up royally with her tours.

Now it was Friday afternoon and there was no way she was going anywhere but home tonight. The door swung open and she glanced over to see Claire enter. Her friend looked determined, and Tammy squared her shoulders in a defensive move.

"Hey, Claire," she said in greeting.

She made a move to pass her and Claire gripped her arm. "Hold it right there."

"What?"

"What?" Claire crossed her arms, blocking her exit. "What the hell is going on with you? That's what."

"I don't know what you're talking about."

"You don't? Have you seen Ben?"

At the mention of his name, she gave a jerk. "I'm not seeing

Ben anymore."

"I know. That's not what I mean. I meant, have you seen what he looks like?"

Of course she had. He looked hot, and strong, and sweet. And like everything she could ever want.

"What does he look like?" she asked Claire.

"He looks like you. Miserable."

"That's not my problem." Tammy lifted her chin. "He's a big boy. He'll get over this."

"Maybe. Will you?"

"There's nothing to get over, really. We had a good time. It's over. End of story."

Claire shook her head. "Nope. I'm not buying it. Something happened. I caught you crying in your office last Monday, Tammy. And all week you've been dragging your perfect little butt all around the office."

"Claire, I can't talk about this."

"Not even to me?"

Tears choked Tammy's throat. "Especially not to you."

Claire's face mirrored the sadness in Tammy's heart. "Why not? I thought we were friends."

That did it. Hormones, best friend, baby. It was too much.

She burst into loud tears and hugged Claire so tight she thought she would break her.

"My God." Claire held on just as tight, stroking a hand over Tammy's hair. "What is it?"

"I'm pregnant," Tammy whispered.

Claire stilled, and then held her back. "You're pregnant?"

Tammy sniffed, nodding. "Yes."

"Why couldn't you tell me?"

Tammy wiped at her cheeks, shaking her head. "I know how hard you've been trying, Claire. I didn't want to tell you because I felt like I'd stolen something."

Claire held a hand to her chest, her face shining. "You can't steal what I don't have, Tammy. I'm not having a baby yet, but I will. I promise you that."

"But I never wanted this," Tammy said.

"So?"

"So?" Tammy gaped at her. "That's it? So?"

"Yeah. You're having a baby. You're a big girl. I've never seen you give up so easily. Why would you now?"

"Give up on what?"

Claire beamed at her. "On a future with Ben! I assume he's the father."

Tammy slanted her a look. "Yes, funny girl."

"Well, what did he say when you told him?"

Tammy looked away.

"Tammy Donato, tell me you told him he's going to be a father."

"I didn't." She held up her hands. "I couldn't. He was spouting stuff about a future and that maybe he has feelings for me and it was all just too much." She sniffed again. "And not enough."

Claire gave a sage nod. "You love him."

"I don't know if I love him," Tammy said.

"That's bullshit, and you know it. You love him."

Tammy hiccupped. "Maybe I do, but that doesn't matter."

Claire grabbed her shoulder. "Didn't you tell me just a few weeks ago that you didn't want to get involved with him because he was forever?"

"Something like that."

Claire glanced down toward Tammy's belly, and then back up at her. "Seems to me that forever bit you right on the butt. What are you going to do about it?"

"But Ben doesn't know he's forever," Tammy said. "He insists he's not, and then he wants to 'see where this goes,' whatever the hell that means."

Claire stepped back. "God, you're both so stupid."

"Hey." Tammy pointed to herself. "Expectant mother here."

"Look. It seems to me you've both been running away from what's right in front of you. You don't have to lose this, Tammy. If you woman-up, you might get everything you've always wanted."

"I've never wanted this," she said, sounding a lot less sure of that than she'd ever been.

"I don't believe that for a second."

"It's so messy, Claire. All of it."

"So?"

"Again, with so?" Tammy blew out a breath. "I didn't think I wanted this little ravioli but it's here now. And I do want it."

"Little ravioli?" Claire smiled. "How cute is that?"

Tammy found a smile. "Never mind."

"Maybe what you have with Ben is here now, too."

Tammy shook her head. "It's not. He's not sure he's even hanging around here. He lives at the B and B, for God's sake."

"So?"

Tammy threw up her hands. "God, you're impossible."

Claire suddenly hugged her again. "You're having a baby!"

294

She leaned back and grinned. "Do you realize how gorgeous this kid will be?"

"Of course." Tammy smiled. "But don't get ahead of yourself. There's no way Ben will want this baby, gorgeous or not."

"And why the hell not?" Claire snapped.

Tammy's heart warmed. Claire was outraged on her behalf.

"Down, girl," Tammy said. "I'm just saying that I might have been avoiding him all week but it was pretty darn easy. He's been avoiding me, too. What does that tell you?"

"That you're both idiots?"

Tammy laughed. "Thanks, girlfriend. You make me feel better." She held up a hand. "But you can't tell Jake anything about this."

"Why not?"

"He'll tell Ben. Don't even try to tell me he won't."

"Oh, he totally would. He wouldn't be able to stop himself."

"He and Ben are pretty close." Tammy thought for a second. "Ben's a part of the family, no matter what he says."

"He says he isn't?" Claire looked a little hurt. "I think of him like I think of Rick."

Tammy shrugged. "Ben's issues aren't my problem. I have

other things on my mind."

Claire grinned again.

"And lose that smile, Claire," Tammy said. "Everybody will know something's up."

Claire's expression sobered. "Ollie hasn't said anything?"

"I think Ollie's afraid I'm going to cry all over him if he asks me a thing."

"Okay." Claire hugged her again. "You'll figure it out, Tammy. You're a smart cookie."

"Coming from you, that's high praise."

Claire shrugged. "Just promise me you'll talk to him?"

"I can't promise that. I'll *think* about talking to him, though. Good enough?"

Claire rolled her eyes. "I guess."

Tammy left the ladies' room and headed back to her office to pick up her stuff. She planned nothing more this weekend than hiding out at home. No Chapman barbeques or getting sun on the beach. She and the cooking channel were going to be very close friends.

Friends. She had Claire in her corner. Despite the fact that Tammy had what she so desperately wanted, she'd made it clear she had her back. She and the little ravioli would be okay.

"You hear that?" she asked her belly. "We're going to okay."

As for the rest of it, she so wasn't going there.

***

"What crawled up your ass?"

Ben looked up from his beer to see his brother Jake scowling at him.

"What?" he asked.

Jake raised his brows. "You've been sulking and snapping all week, bro."

"Sorry," Ben grumbled.

They sat on the front porch of Jake and Claire's house, facing the green space across the street. Claire had gone into St. Cloud to see her dad, so Jake was on his own this Saturday afternoon. Ben was lucky his brother had called him to hang out. He'd needed to do something with himself after the week he'd had.

"You know you can tell me anything, right?" Jake asked.

Ben studied him for a minute. "I can?"

Anger showed briefly on his brother's face. "What the hell do I have to do, Ben? Don't you get it by now?"

"Get what?"

"You're family, bro. Whether you like it or not. Christ."

"I like it, Jake. I'm sorry. It's taken me a while to figure this all out."

"Figure what out? We were all blindsided by Bill's news. What makes you so special?"

"I don't think I'm special."

"You're not an only child anymore," Jake said. "Big deal."

"I don't miss that. I care about all of you."

"Yeah, yeah."

Ben set his beer down on the decking and faced Jake. "I'm sorry I've been such a dick all week. Me and Tammy... Well, there is no more me and Tammy."

"Was there ever?"

Ben shrugged. "Damned if I know. We both wanted the same thing, in the beginning. I don't know how I fucked it up."

"Because you were thinking with your dick, bro."

"How can you say that? I thought Tammy and I could be friends, too."

Jake shook his head. "That would never be enough for you."

Ben stared at him. "You don't even know me."

Jake smirked. "Dude, I *am* you. Or at least I was until I had the good sense to fall for Claire. At first I just wanted her." Jake took a long draw of his beer, and then shot Ben a crooked smile. "Good thing she loves me."

"It's different with me and Tammy."

"Tell yourself that."

"It doesn't matter anyway. She ended it when I mentioned maybe wanting more."

"Maybe?" Jake's eyes went wide. "Jesus, you said *maybe*?"

"Yeah. So?"

"God, you're so stupid."

"Huh?"

"She loves you, Ben."

Ben gave himself a split second to think about that. "No way. It must be the beer talking."

"She loves you," Jake went on. "That's the only explanation for her pulling away and giving you the cold shoulder all week."

"What do you know about it?"

"I only know that Claire said you're both avoiding each other."

"And that means love? Then you can have it."

"I do. I can't tell you how great it is without growing a pair of breasts, but I couldn't stand to live without Claire."

"We're different. Or, we were."

"Mmm-hmm. Friend zone and then, bam!"

Ben froze. "Yeah. Something like that."

"You need to figure out what you want."

"I don't *want* anything." Ben pulled another beer out of the cooler set between their chairs. "Whatever. She doesn't want it and I'm not going to push it."

Jake shrugged. "Seems to me you're making a mistake there."

"Maybe."

"And there's that word again." Jake grinned. "You have to do something about that."

Ben found a smile. "Okay, cards on the table?"

"Just you and me out here, bro."

Ben took a breath. "I think I love her." When Jake raised his brows again, Ben bit back a curse. "Okay, I love her. Happy?"

"Yeah. But you're not."

"No. I'm not."

"Figure this out, man. Tammy's one of the hottest women around. She's not going to be single for long."

"Why? What do you know? Is she seeing someone?"

"No. Not yet, anyway. She's never dated much, from what I can tell. You're the first."

Ben sat back. "Seriously?"

"There's something there for her too, Ben. There has to be."

He thought about how weird she'd been at the office. About how sad she'd looked a couple of times in his room that last night. The way she'd loved him and wrung him dry.

"Do you really think she loves me?" Ben asked his brother.

"Only one way to find out."

A shiver went up Ben's spine. "I've never had that conversation before."

"Man up, bro."

"You make it sound so easy."

"It's anything but easy. Worth it, though."

Jake's simple words broke through to him. It was easy, loving Tammy. He had no idea how to prove it, though.

He stood. "I have to use the can."

Jake waved at the front door. "Go for it. Do some thinking while you're in there."

Ben punched him in the arm and went into the house. Afterwards he was walking back toward the front of the house when Claire's voice reached him. She was talking on her phone and her head was down.

"I'll go with you on Monday, Tammy."

301

He froze and turned around. Claire still hadn't seen him, she was so focused on her phone call.

"It's your first doctor's visit. I'm going with you."

Coldness settled in his belly. Was Tammy sick? Was that what was wrong with her?

"Why is Tammy going to the doctor?" he asked.

Claire's head shot up, surprise clear on her face. "I've gotta go," she said into the phone. "I'll call you tonight."

She ended the call and held the phone behind her like that could hide the fact that she'd been on a call with Tammy.

"Hey, Ben."

"Why is Tammy going to the doctor?" he asked again.

Claire blushed to the roots of her hair. "I can't say."

"What's wrong? Tell me, Claire."

She pulled back at his intensity. "Ben, I…" She looked over his shoulder, her face registering relief. "Jake."

"What's up?" Jake asked.

Ben turned to him. "Why is Tammy going to the doctor, Jake?"

"How the hell would I know?"

They both turned back to Claire. She hung her head. "She's going to kill me."

Fear crawled up Ben's spine. "Tell me, Claire. I need to know."

A light came into Claire's eyes as she stared at him hard. "Why, Ben? Why do you need to know?"

He looked at Jake, who apparently had nothing to offer, and then back at Claire. "Because I love her."

A smile broke out on Claire's face. "I knew it!"

Ben blinked. "What?"

"I knew it! You see, Jake? I knew it!"

Ben fisted his hands. "Tell me, damn it."

"Tammy's pregnant, Ben," she said.

The floor dipped beneath him and he felt his brother grab on to his shoulder.

"Pregnant." Ben couldn't seem to make sense of the word. "She's pregnant."

Jake gave him a squeeze. "Way to go, bro."

Ben looked at him, seeing the grin on his brother's face. "Pregnant," he said again.

"Yes, and you're the proud papa," Claire said. "Now what are you going to do about it?"

Claire looked fierce but she didn't scare him. He knew what he was going to do. Finally.

"I'm going to make her see how perfect we are together."

"About damn time," Jake said.

Ben waved a hand and headed out the door. "Is she home?" he asked as he neared the door.

"She sure is," Claire answered.

Ben got in his Jeep and drove to Tammy's townhouse. When he got there he sat for a minute. What the hell was he going to say to her?

"Are you going to sit out there all day?"

He looked over to find Tammy standing on her porch.

He got out of the car and walked up to her. "How did you know I was coming?"

She held up her phone and he knew Claire had given her a heads-up. "Girl code," she said.

He rolled his eyes. "Women. Okay, so Claire told you I was coming over. What else did she tell you?"

"Not much. Just that you have something to tell me?"

"I do."

"It better not be more of that 'us' stuff, Ben. Not if you're only thinking their *might* be an 'us.'"

"There's an 'us,' all right." He stepped up and wrapped his arms around her. "I know it's real, Tammy. We're real."

304

"We are?"

He nodded. "And that's not all I know."

She gasped. "You know about the little ravioli," she said softly.

"The what?"

"The baby, Ben."

He chuckled. "Ravioli, huh? I like it."

She shrugged, ducking her head. "Okay."

"I love you, Tammy."

Her head shot up so fast she bumped his chin. He bit his tongue, but he didn't care. The hope on her face took his breath.

"You love me?" she asked.

He nodded. "And you love me."

She scoffed. "You think so, Big Ben?"

He grinned. "I know so. I want us to be a family, Tammy. I like being part of a family, and I want that with you."

"Well, look at you." She smiled as she came up on tiptoes to wrap her arms around his neck the way he liked. "I won the prize, I think."

"We both did. Marry me?"

"Whoa." Her eyes searched his face, wide and sparkling. "Slow down there."

"Why? This little ravioli isn't going to wait."

She laughed and hugged him tighter. "Okay, then. That was easy."

"Easy?" He shook his head. "No way. Worth it? Definitely."

She laughed again and kissed him, and he felt it to his soul.

Epilogue

Ben stood in front of the Craftsman house he'd designed. The first home built for the new development. It had already won a design award and was gaining attention for being a classic style with a modern sensibility while staying ecologically sound. There was even talk that a few architectural magazines wanted to feature the house, on their covers and in their pages. All of that was pretty damn good, but none of it was what he liked most about it.

The house wasn't being used as a model, as originally planned. He'd made that decision right after holding Tammy in his arms after she'd agreed to marry him, and Mr. Forbes hadn't balked when Ben informed him of the change. No. This was their house. Their home. A place to grow their family, starting with their little ravioli.

"What are you thinking about, Big Ben?" Tammy asked, gliding up to him in her sexy, professional work clothes.

He wrapped an arm around her waist. "I'm thinking about how I can't wait to fill all those rooms."

She laughed softly. "Hey, I'm not one of my sisters." Her hand settled on the tiny bump showing through the front of her skirt. "Let's just try this one on for size and I'll think about a second."

He nodded. "Fair enough."

She cuddled closer and he breathed in her flowers-and-spice scent.

"My mother wants us to go up to Jersey for Thanksgiving," she said.

He made a face of mock horror. "A Donato holiday?"

She nudged him with her hip. "Oh, you love my family."

"I had no choice. They descended on Cypress like locusts for our wedding. They're kind of irresistible, you know."

"Like me?" she asked, her head tilted to one side.

He growled and grabbed her in a hug, not caring what the few neighbors thought. "Not like you. Nobody's like you."

"You better believe it."

Heat flared between them. It still burned so hot he sometimes thought he might be fantasizing. But she was real. This was real. He would have the family he never even knew he wanted. His brothers and sister. His nephew and maybe more little Chapmans. His own little Chapman.

"At least we'll miss Bill's visit," he said.

She shook her head. "I still can't believe your brother

invited him for Thanksgiving."

Ben shrugged. "Rick surprised the hell out of me with that one, too. Bill's been on his best behavior since the wedding. Makes me wonder what he's up to."

"Don't borrow trouble, Ben."

He wasn't going to waste another minute thinking about his father. That was for sure. He had more pleasant things to occupy his thoughts. Besides, if Bill hadn't sent him to Cypress he wouldn't have found what he didn't even know he'd been looking for.

It was true that he had no idea what he wanted when he'd come down here, only that he wasn't happy with what he had before. Not in his career or in his personal life. He'd managed to figure it out though, only screwing up a couple of times before recognizing the winning cards in his hand. He couldn't keep the grin off his face if he tried.

"Now, there's that dimple," she laughed.

He just hugged her tighter. He didn't care if he had no poker face. He'd have it all and Tammy too. He was a lucky bastard and even if Tammy ever let him forget it, he never would.

He'd won it all.

About the Author

JoMarie DeGioia is a bestselling author of Historical and Contemporary Romance. She's known Mickey Mouse from the "inside," has been a copyeditor for her tiny town's newspaper, and a bookseller. A hybrid author, she also writes Young Adult Fantasy/Adventure stories, New Adult Romance and Paranormal Romance. She gets lost in DIY projects around the house and works out plot ideas during long runs. She divides her time between Central Florida and New England.

Discover books by JoMarie DeGioia

The Dashing Nobles series, including
More Than Passion
Pride and Fire
Just Perfect
More Than Charming
The Cypress Corners series, including
Finding Harmony
Taming Jake
Loving Cassie
The Gifted YA Fantasy/Adventure Trilogy,
including Gifted

The Baunachs of the Dell Series, including
Luke's Gold

Connect with me online

Twitter: https://twitter.com/JoMarieDeGioia

Facebook:
https://www.facebook.com/JoMarie.DeGioia.Author

Website: www.jomariedegioia.com